Althou̶...
the nota...
snappec...

He stood and found himself over on Lydia's driveway before he even realized what he was doing there. Taking hold of Sim by the back of his shirt collar, he yanked him away from her.

"I believe the lady wants you to back off."

She nodded, and after tossing the other man a look of mild disdain, she hurried up the steps to the porch, unlocked her front door and disappeared into the house.

When Alec glanced back at Sim, he was already heading toward his Lincoln, muttering under his breath. He got in, closed the door, and pealed out of the driveway.

"Hey, little man," Alec said as if the guy could hear him, "you're doing it all wrong. You've got to sweet talk a woman into a good night kiss, not act like an ogre."

Shaking his head, Alec watched the car take off down the dimly lit street, simultaneously wondering if he'd be able to get a good night kiss out of Lydia Boswick on a first date. Bet he could. . .

ANDREA BOESHAAR was born and raised in Milwaukee, Wisconsin. Married for over twenty years, she and her husband, Daniel, have three adult sons. Andrea has been writing for over thirteen years, but writing exclusively for the Christian market for eight. Writing is something she loves to share as well as help others develop. Andrea recently quit her job to stay home, take care of her family, and write. Check out Andrea's web page at http://members.aol.com/akbwrites2

HEARTSONG PRESENTS

Books under the pen name Andrea Shaar
HP79—An Unwilling Warrior

Books by Andrea Boeshaar
HP188—An Uncertain Heart
HP238—Annie's Song
HP270—Promise Me Forever
HP279—An Unexpected Love
HP301—Second Time Around
HP342—The Haven of Rest
HP359—An Undaunted Faith

Southern Sympathies

Andrea Boeshaar

Heartsong Presents

To my son, Brian, who reads my work and always has an encouraging word to say about it afterwards.

And special thanks to Traci DePree, copy editor extraordinaire.

A note from the author:
I love to hear from my readers! You may correspond with me by writing: **Andrea Boeshaar**
Author Relations
PO Box 719
Uhrichsville, OH 44683

ISBN 1-57748-955-1

SOUTHERN SYMPATHIES

Woodruff, North Carolina is a fictitious town and a product of the author's imagination.

All of the characters and events in this book are fictitious. Any resemblance to actual persons, living or dead, or to actual events is purely coincidental.

Cover illustration by Chris Cocozza.

PRINTED IN THE U.S.A.

one

Sixty-five degrees and sunny! With a smile, Alec Corbett gazed up at the clear blue North Carolina sky. *Sure wouldn't see this kind of weather in Wisconsin on the last weekend of January*, he mused. *Then, again, you never know. Wisconsin weather is about as fickle as a woman!*

Walking toward the house he'd just purchased, Alec tried not to let his thoughts stray. No use dwelling on the past—a past that included an engagement gone bad and one whimsical woman named Denise Lisinski.

Don't think about her, he admonished himself, pulling the keys from his blue jeans pocket. *Too nice a day to think about Denise.*

Standing on the small front porch, Alec could hear the wind rustling through the treetops of the quiet neighborhood. There weren't any sidewalks such as he was accustomed to after years of big-city living. Only a simple asphalt road that meandered down the block.

Alec glanced across the narrow strip of lawn that served as a dividing line between his property and his neighbor's. And, although he was quite content with his own place—a low-maintenance ranch-styled home encased in a combination of brown brick and tan aluminum—he had to admit an aesthetic appreciation of the older, two-story red brick house next door. White shutters framed the home's windows facing the street while the front entrance was graced with a huge cement porch, complete with massive white pillars.

Well, look at that, he thought, spying the wooden swing hanging at the end of the portico. He could suddenly envision two lovers sitting there together, talking, sharing their most intimate thoughts.

Whoa, I gotta quit thinking like some heartsick schoolboy, he berated himself. *I'm not engaged to Denise anymore. I'm not getting married. I'm moving into this house today, in a different town, a different state—*

"Hey, Alec! Should we start unloading the truck now? I backed it into the driveway."

He turned at the sound of his friend's voice. Tim Parker and four other men from church had volunteered to help him move today. "Yeah, sure," he called back. "I'll open up and we can start hauling furniture."

Alec unlocked the door and walked in. The air in the living room felt cool and still—the calm before the moving-in storm. Quickly roaming from room to room, he mentally placed all his belongings in various sites. His bedroom set in here, the extra double bed in a guest room there, and an office where he could set up his computer in the smallest of the three bedrooms. He chuckled, thinking that in a matter of minutes this one-story ranch home would be a whirlwind of activity.

"Okay, where do you want 'em?" Tim asked, carrying in two matching lamps while his glasses slid slightly down his nose.

Alec strode purposely to the front door. "Those can stay here in the living room."

"Hey, Alec," dark-headed Larry Matthews asked, holding one end of a dresser while Rick Stevens held the other, "where do you want this?"

"Master bedroom. Go down the hallway. . .to the right. That's it."

Alec sighed. It was going to be a long, but very exciting day. Moving into this house meant the start of a new life for him!

❧

"Boy, he's sure gottalotta junk!" eight-year-old Tyler Boswick declared as he watched his new neighbor move in. He peered down at his younger sister, Brooke, who stood on the fence beside him. "I hope he's got some kids."

"Me, too. And I hope he's got a girl my age." Her brown eyes grew wide. "Here he comes again, Ty, ask him."

"Okay. . . Hey, mister," he called. The man headed for the moving truck stopped and looked over at them expectantly. "Are y'all the one moving in?"

"Yep, that's me."

Tyler considered him, noticing his straw-colored short hair and tough-looking features. He had the rugged face of an army man he'd once seen on TV. His interest shifted to the man's clothing—faded blue T-shirt and dirty jeans. They were hard-working clothes, by the looks of them. *Yeah,* Ty decided, *he just might be a dad.*

"Well, I was just wondering," he proceeded, undaunted, "do y'all have any kids our age?"

"Nope. Sorry."

Dashing all of Tyler's hopes in a mere fraction of a second, the man continued on his way.

"Do you have any kids at all?" Brooke asked hopefully. "A little girl like me, maybe?"

Pausing and turning toward them again, the man shook his head and grinned. Tyler thought he appeared a lot friendlier when he smiled. "No, I don't have any kids. I'm not married."

Brooke frowned. "That's too bad."

He chuckled. "Depends on how you look at it."

Tyler exchanged puzzled glances with his sister. Then they both shrugged simultaneously and watched the man walk up the ramp into the moving truck and come back out.

"He sure is strong," Brooke remarked.

"Aw, that's nothing," Tyler said, unwilling to admit that carrying four kitchen chairs, two looped through each arm, was fairly impressive. "Men can carry lots of heavy things at once."

"Not Grampa," Brook countered. "He only carries his Bible."

"That's cuz he's a preacher of a whole big church, dodo bird. He gets other people to carry all his heavy stuff."

Brooke narrowed her eyes at him. "Don't call me 'dodo' or I'm telling Mama."

"Go ahead," Tyler replied, lifting his chin stubbornly. "But if you tell, we'll have to go in."

Brooke clamped her mouth shut. Neither of them wanted to go inside for the night and he knew it. And if little tattletale Brooke told their mother, they'd have to go in early for their Saturday-night baths.

Both children looked on curiously as two other men emerged, walked into the truck, then reappeared, wheeling a refrigerator toward the house. Next, their new neighbor carried in a stove, aided by another of his friends. But minutes later, he showed up again with nothing more than a can of cola in one hand. Much to Tyler's surprise, he sauntered over to them.

"Are y'all gonna holler at us for standing on the fence?" Brooke inquired, her voice quivering slightly. "Mr. Smith used to holler at us."

"Naw, I'm not going to do that," the man said, sitting on the corner of the picnic table that a couple of men had put in the wide backyard hours before. "I don't care if you stand on it. I think that fence has seen better days, anyway." He eyed them speculatively. "What are your names?"

"I'm Tyler Michael Boswick. And this is my sister, Brooke Elizabeth Boswick."

The man grinned. "Glad to meet you, Tyler. . .Brooke. I'm Alec."

"Mr. Alec?" Brooke asked uncertainly.

"No. Alec Corbett. But you can call me by my first name."

"Oh no, sir, we can't!" Brooke informed him, shaking her blond head vigorously. "Mama says it's *dispectful* to call a grown-up by his first name."

"She means 'disrespectful,' " Tyler said informatively. "She's only five."

"Almost six," Brooke corrected him.

Tyler shrugged, unimpressed. "I'm almost nine."

Mr. Alec smiled. "Have you two lived here a long time?"

"All our lives," Tyler replied. "What about you?"

"I'm from Milwaukee, Wisconsin, but now Woodruff, North Carolina, is my home."

"Hmm. Well, my best friend, Matt Smith, used to live in your house, but he moved."

"Guess he had to, huh?"

"Uh-huh. His dad got another job. . .all the way in Charlotte."

"That's not so far away."

"Yes, it is," Tyler replied as memories of his friend's moving day resurfaced. That had been the saddest day in all his life.

"I'm going to work in Charlotte starting this week," Mr. Alec said. "I'll be making the drive every day. Takes about a half-hour, more or less, depending on the weather and traffic. No big deal, buddy."

Tyler's jaw dropped. "You work all the way in Charlotte, Tennessee? And you live *here*?"

Mr. Alec threw his head back and laughed loudly. It was such a happy sound that it made Tyler smile. "No, no," he said between chortles. "I work over in Charlotte—*North Carolina.*"

"Oh, yeah." Tyler chuckled, too. He'd forgotten about *that* Charlotte.

"Oh, yeah," Mr. Alec mimicked, smiling all the while. "And where, may I ask, is Charlotte, Tennessee?"

"Um. . ." Tyler thought for a few moments, trying to remember what he'd heard the grown-ups say. At last he sighed. "I dunno where it is, but I know it's not around here!"

"Tennessee is just the next state over."

"Uh-huh." Tyler nodded, but inside he knew he'd never see Matt again. Tennessee might as well have been on the other side of the world. He wasn't sure what had happened, but something had—something bad. And that was why Mr. Smith got another job and moved away. Far away.

"So where does your dad work?" Mr. Alec wanted to know.

"We don't have a daddy," Brooke informed him with a sad expression. "He died when I was three."

"I'm sorry to hear that."

"But he's in heaven, so it's okay," Tyler quickly added. "And Mama doesn't cry so much anymore. Hardly at all, even."

"That's good. . .I guess."

Tyler watched as Mr. Alec took a gulp of his cola. He wondered what his grandfather would think of this man. Grampa Boswick always said that it was rude to drink straight out of a can. Gentlemen used a drinking glass.

"So, do you guys go to church?"

"Uh-huh," Brooke said, nodding. "Mama says we all but live at church."

"Is that right?" Mr. Alec chuckled again, and Tyler got the feeling his new neighbor liked kids a whole lot more than he let on.

"Mama works at church," Brooke said. "She's a secatary."

"Secretary?" Mr. Alec grinned.

"Yep. And our grampa is the pastor."

"Which church?"

"Southern Pride Community Church," Tyler replied. "We call it SPCC for short."

"Hmm. . ." Their new neighbor got a thoughtful look on his face. "Is that the big church off the highway between here and King's Mountain?"

"I think so," Tyler said, wonderingly. He'd have to ask Mama later to be sure.

"It is," Brooke piped in.

"Aw, you don't know."

"Uh-huh. I see the sign that says *King's Mountain* every day on the way to school." She turned to Mr. Alec with a sweet expression—the very one that always made their mama go easier on her when they both got in trouble. "Our school is in the same place as our church."

"I think I know the school you mean."

Tyler didn't reply, but it irritated him that his little sister seemed to know something he didn't. Maybe he'd have to pay more attention on the way to church tomorrow.

"Tyler! Brooke!" Their mother's soft voice floated over to them from where she stood on the back porch. "Time to come in now."

"Rats!" Tyler grumbled.

"Comin', Mama," Brooke replied, jumping down off the fence. She was acting like a goody-two-shoes and it annoyed Tyler to no end!

Mr. Alec stood up and stretched. "Well, I guess my break is over, too. Nice meeting you, Tyler."

"Thanks, but you can call me Ty. All my friends do."

The man laughed. "Okay, *Ty*. I guess we'll be seeing each other around."

"I reckon so." Tyler hopped off the fence and walked as slowly as he could toward the door, where his mother still stood waiting for him. He even stopped to pick up an old, worn-out penny from the driveway, but, much to Tyler's dismay, she didn't go on inside ahead of him.

"Come on, Ty, hurry up. Your bath is getting cold."

He grimaced. "Can't Brooke go first?"

His mother raised her eyebrow in reply and he knew he'd better not fuss—when Mama raised her brow, she meant business!

He trudged up the back steps. "Yes, ma'am," he muttered, walking past her into the house.

"Who were you and Brooke talking to?"

"Mr. Alec Corbett," he answered, perking up a bit. Maybe if he talked about the new neighbor, his mother would forget about the bath. "He's real nice, Mama, and he told Brooke and me to call him Mr. Alec for short."

"So he's the one who bought the Smiths' house. I'd been wondering who was moving in all day."

"Yep, it's him." Tyler watched as his mother threw one last glance out the back door before closing it tightly. "He's certainly a big man, isn't he?"

"Sure is. He's really strong, too," Brooke stated informatively.

"Oh?"

"Yes, but he talks kinda funny." She wrinkled her nose just like she did whenever Mama made something different for supper.

"Where's he from?"

"Milwaukee, Wisconsin," Tyler replied with a puzzled frown. "Where is that, anyhow?"

Mama smiled, making her blue-gray eyes shine. "I'll show you on the map hanging on your bedroom wall right before bedtime—*after* your bath."

Tyler groaned, ignoring the amused expression on his mother's face. Why did she have to remember *everything*?

"Does Mr. Alec have a family?" she asked, steering him toward the bathroom.

"Nope. Just him." Tyler paused, wishing the knot in his throat would go away. "No kids. . ."

"Oh, I'm so sorry, honey. I know how disappointed you must be."

Mama captured him in an embrace, drawing him to her slim body, which always smelled as good as the summer flower garden she planted every year behind the house. Then she kissed his cheek. "At least you'll always have Jesus," she whispered near his ear. "Jesus will never leave you."

Suddenly Tyler felt like crying. He wiggled out of his mother's arms since he didn't want her to see. "I better go take my bath," he muttered.

Grabbing hold of the bottom of his T-shirt, he pulled it up over his head as he entered the bathroom. He shut the door and, while he finished undressing, he tried not to think of how Matt Smith had moved away forever and how a grown-up had taken over his best friend's house next door.

two

Lydia Boswick peered out her kitchen window as she finished cleaning up the supper dishes. Lights glowed from the house next door and seeing them caused her heart to ache for her dear friend Sherry Smith. They'd been close for years, chatting over cups of coffee and helping each other out with their kids. When Michael died, Sherry had been such a comfort to Lydia. But then the Smiths abandoned their faith, according to Lydia's father-in-law, and they'd all but turned their backs on their brothers and sisters in Christ at Southern Pride Community Church. Sherry stopped talking to Lydia right after Christmas; and, though it had been the death of a friendship as opposed to a husband, it hurt almost as much as losing Michael. And losing her mother, even though Mama wasn't dead—physically, anyway.

Don't think about her now, she chastened herself. *Mama made her decisions. Now she has to live with them. . .and so do I.*

Pushing aside her tumultuous thoughts, Lydia chanced one last look through the blue-and-white-checked curtains adorning the little window above her kitchen sink. She could see the backyard next door and the five men who sat around a picnic table. Weren't they freezing? Since sundown, the temperatures had fallen into the fifties. Lydia wondered if they were drinking alcoholic beverages and, therefore, had become numb to the cold. Adding soap, closing the dishwasher, and turning on the machine, she silently dreaded being a neighbor to a single man who had nothing better to do than party with his friends all night long.

"Mama, it's eight o'clock," Tyler hollered from upstairs. "Are you coming to hear our prayers?"

"I'm on my way," she called in reply.

Lydia glanced around her kitchen to be sure she hadn't left some task undone. *Now to get those kids to bed.*

"Mama, come hear my prayers first," Brooke insisted.

The girl grabbed Lydia's hand just as she reached the upper hallway, pulling her mother toward her bedroom. Brooke's bright blond hair shone from its scrubbing earlier that evening. She was dressed for bed in her pink nightie, and Lydia thought her daughter resembled a life-sized, huggable, kissable doll. She could hardly refuse the request. Besides, Tyler wouldn't mind if Brooke said her prayers first. Glancing across the hall and into his bedroom, Lydia spied him playing on the computer his grampa Boswick purchased for him a couple of months ago as a Christmas gift.

Lydia followed Brooke into her room. Tucking her in, she sat on the edge of the twin bed that was draped in a pink, lacy comforter and heaped with stuffed animals. "There's hardly room for you in this bed," Lydia remarked with a smile.

"That's cuz Grampa keeps buying me all these aminals." Brooke grabbed a sweet-faced lion and hugged it tightly. "I love 'em."

"I know you do, sweetheart."

"And I named every one. . .just like Adam got to name all the aminals that God gave him. This one's name is Mr. Lion."

"That's very original," Lydia said teasingly, although the humor was lost on the five-year-old.

"We're learning about Adam and Eve in Sunday school."

"That's right." Kissing her daughter's forehead, Lydia was suddenly reminded of the lesson she had to prepare for the ladies' Bible study she taught right before the Sunday morning service the next day. "All right, say your prayers now."

Brooke squeezed her eyes closed and then folded her hands over Mr. Lion. "God bless Grampa Boswick and Gramma Boswick, Gramma Reimer—" She paused. "What's her new name again? I forgot."

"Jackson," Lydia reminded her daughter as another little

piece of her heart crumbled. "She's Gramma Jackson now."

Brooke nodded. "And God bless Gramma Jackson, Mama, Tyler. . .and me."

She peeked at Lydia, who raised a questioning brow. "That's not much of a prayer."

"I know, 'cept it's all I can think of right now."

"Very well," Lydia conceded, bestowing one last kiss on Brooke's cheek and wishing her a good night's sleep. "You can talk to Jesus any time, not just when I'm listening to your bedtime prayers."

The little girl nodded once more.

Smiling, Lydia shut off the lamp beside Brooke's bed and left the room, closing the door behind her.

"Tyler, time to turn off that computer," she announced, crossing the hallway.

"Aw, do I have to?"

"Yes."

"But I'm trying to see if Matt's E-mail still works."

"It probably doesn't."

"I'm almost done typing the letter. . . ."

"Okay. Finish up, but make it quick. You can type a longer message once you find out if Matt has the same on-line address."

The boy smiled, turned back to the computer screen, and continued his "hunt-and-peck" method of typing out a message to his friend.

Sitting down on the end of Tyler's bed, Lydia surveyed her son's room. Blue and green plaid walls surrounded the heavy mahogany furniture that had once belonged to Michael when he was a child.

Michael. Oddly enough, thinking about him didn't hurt nearly as badly as it once did. She could even talk about him now and his freak heart attack without choking on her emotions and tears. Dead at the age of thirty-four. Who would have ever guessed it? Not Michael's parents, who'd never known about their only son's rare heart condition, one that had gone undetected until the autopsy. Not Lydia, who was crazy in love with the tall, blond, handsome young man whom she'd met right after she and her mother joined Southern Pride Community Church.

She'd been just sixteen years old at the time. He was twenty, refined, educated, and mature. They were immediately and obviously attracted to each other, and they fell hopelessly in love. While the Boswicks encouraged Michael to marry a slew of other young ladies—those closer to his age—Michael had waited determinedly for Lydia, even though they'd been separated while he went to college and law school. Then finally they were married the day after her twenty-first birthday. Tyler arrived three years later and Brooke, three years after him. Life had been perfectly blissful. . .until Michael died.

"Okay, I'm done," Tyler said, causing Lydia to snap out of her reminiscing.

He jumped into bed and dove under the sheets, ruffling the light blue comforter. Smiling, Lydia tousled his hair. Both children had inherited their father's coloring, blond hair with deep brown eyes. Her heart used to ache just looking at them, remembering her beloved husband each and every time she did so. But time was a healer of wounds and though Lydia once thought she'd never get over the pain of losing Michael, it had dulled to the point of being tolerable. She'd even been able to counsel a new widow at church, another sign that she was healing.

"Thank you, God, for bringing me and my family through another day," Tyler began. "Please bless Grampa and Gramma Boswick. . . ."

As her son continued to say his routine bedtime prayers, Lydia's thoughts strayed and time after time she had to force herself to concentrate on what he was saying. She still had much to do before she could call it a night.

"And please, God, give me a new bike."

That got her attention. "Tyler. . .?"

"Well, my birthday is coming up on May first. I just wanna

make sure God has plenty of time to get it."

Lydia made a *tsk* sound with her tongue. "You have a bike."

"I know. But I want a mountain bike—like the one Matt got at Christmas."

Shaking her head, Lydia thought her son had more toys than he could possibly ever need—and then some! "Tyler, we should pray for people who don't have all the nice things we do. There are children right here in the United States who don't have a place to sleep tonight. They're poor and home-less. But look at you. . .you're very blessed, all snuggled in a warm, cozy bed with lots of toys around you. It's selfish to ask for more."

Tyler looked quite contrite. "Oh, all right." He closed his eyes and resumed his prayers. "God, if you get me that new bike, I promise I'll give my old one to a poor child."

Lydia shook her head at him, but Tyler kept praying. "And please make that bike a red and black one." Peeking at his mother, he added, "I also ask for all the poor, homeless chil-dren in the world—please find them homes, Lord. I'll even share my bedroom with another boy if You want me to."

The offer touched Lydia's heart, reminding her that Tyler could be very benevolent most of the time.

At last, the boy finished his prayers and Lydia gave him a good-night kiss on the cheek. "Sweet dreams," she murmured as he turned onto his side sleepily.

"Sweet dreams. . ." Then suddenly he sat upright, his fore-head nearly colliding with Lydia's chin.

"Now what?"

"I forgot to ask God something else."

She sighed impatiently, thinking this was one of Ty's many ploys of bedtime procrastination. "All right. Be quick about it."

He closed his eyes. "Dear God, please send me and Brooke a new daddy."

Lydia stifled a gasp of surprise. He'd never prayed for *that* before. Moreover, his voice rang with sincerity.

"He'd have to be a special daddy," Tyler continued, "to take the place of our real daddy who's in heaven. But I know You can do it, God. Amen!" Flopping back against his pillows, the eight-year-old grinned up at her. "Okay, now I can go to sleep."

Startled out of a reply, Lydia could only nod. She walked out of the room and closed the door softly. Taking the stairs slowly, she wondered why her son would ask God for a new daddy. Surely it wasn't because he felt a particular fondness for any certain man. Lydia didn't date, although lately her father-in-law, Gerald Boswick, had been trying to coax her into going out with his attorney, who was also the church's treasurer, Simeon Crenshaw. The only trouble was, Lydia didn't feel interested, and since Gerald wasn't pushing too hard, she politely refused Sim, ignoring the fall bouquet of flowers he'd sent her last Thanksgiving Day and the long-stemmed red roses accompanied by a box of expensive chocolates at Christmas.

I'll have to make a point to question Ty about this new daddy thing tomorrow, she thought, picking up the manila folder off the desk in the living room. Opening it, she pulled out her Bible study notes. She crossed the room and, making herself comfortable in the brightly upholstered, wingback armchair, she began to plan her lesson.

❀

Sunday afternoon shone with promise as Alec drove his sleek black Chevy pickup back home after the worship service and the potluck luncheon that followed. He had visited the small community of Woodruff, North Carolina, several times before actually making the move from Wisconsin, and he'd liked what he'd seen—still did. Life moved at a slower pace down here. Even the fast-food places were slow. But people seemed friendlier and more innocent, to the point that Alec considered them backwards, but in a complimentary way. Who needed big-city sophistication with its high crime rate? Not him. Not anymore. This little "hick town," nestled in the foothills of the Great Smoky Mountains, suited him just right.

Turning into his driveway, Alec sent up a prayer of thanks that he'd so easily found a local church to attend. It was perfect for him, quaint and simple—a reflection of his own personality. And Mark Spencer, the pastor of Berean Baptist Church, was a man with whom Alec's spirit identified. He was a down-to-earth African American whose heart and enthusiasm for people of all races were contagious. A soft-spoken man, Pastor Spencer wasn't flamboyant. His services were filled with practical teachings from God's Word. Even the church building wasn't anything to speak of, with its gray aluminum siding and modest chapel inside, housing metal folding chairs instead of pews. But Alec had learned firsthand that appearances could be deceiving. He refused to judge the congregation solely on its dwelling. He wasn't disappointed, either. Berean's church members turned out to be warm and personable and, just as they'd received him with open arms weeks ago, during his last "just making sure" visit to Woodruff, they'd welcomed him today. Alec appreciated that.

Parking his truck outside the garage, he suddenly thought about his boss, Greg Nivens. Ever since Alec started working at the national firm of Heritage Craft Furniture and Cabinetry, where he labored as a carpenter, Greg had been doing his best to talk Alec into attending his church, Southern Pride Community Church. It was nearer to Charlotte, the same "big city" in which he worked, so right away he wasn't interested. He'd rather stick closer to home. Then the kids next door had mentioned the very same body of believers yesterday. Alec had begun to wonder if maybe the Lord really wanted him there—as if God were giving him hints, leading his thoughts toward SPCC for a special reason. However, Alec got Divine assurance this morning. He was most definitely attending the right church.

Getting out of the garage, he spied the bicycle he'd bought for Denise before she'd broken their engagement. Why had he brought it down here? He should have given it to charity before moving from Wisconsin. Then, again, he hadn't been

thinking straight since Thanksgiving. Heartbreak did that to a
guy, he reasoned. But still, to haul a lousy bike almost a thousand miles. . .

Alec shook his head and continued making his way toward
the house. Childish giggles wafted across the yard, causing
him to pause in his tracks. The boy, Ty, waved from his perch
on the large wooden gym set, and his little sister repeated the
greeting. Alec waved back, smiling and walking the rest of
the way to the house. Those kids sure were cute. He fished in
his trouser pocket for his keys and then thought of Denise's
bike. He couldn't use it—the frame was too small for his
large physique. Why not give it to Tyler? The boy would
probably appreciate it, and Alex wouldn't have to look at it
every time he passed the garage.

"Hey, kid," he called from his small back porch. "Tyler,
come over to the fence. I want to ask you something."

The boy immediately obeyed. "Yes, Mr. Alec?"

"Could you use a bike?"

He shrugged.

"Here, let me show it to you. It's brand new." Alec fetched
it from the garage, and the boy's brown eyes grew as big as
dessert plates.

"Wow! A red-and-black mountain bike! Just what I prayed
for! Mama, Mama," he yelled, turning toward the house
and cupping his mouth with his hands, "come see how God
answered my prayer. Mama, come out here!"

His mother, a petite brunette, stepped out of the back door.
"Tyler, you stop that bellowing. It's rude."

She gave Alec an apologetic look and he smiled. How could
he help but smile? She was lovely, dressed in a long, bluish-
gray dress and matching heels. He watched as she gracefully
stepped to the fence. Her gaze met his and Alec noticed her
eyes were a dusky color—the same hue as her outfit.

"I'm Lydia Boswick," she said in a Southern velvet tone,
offering her right hand. "I see you've met my children."

Alec took her hand, keenly aware of how small and cool it

felt in his. "Yes. . ." It was the most intelligent reply he could think of.

"Mama, Mr. Alec is giving me this bike. Look!"

Alec released her hand and gave the woman an embarrassed grin. "Bought it for someone who didn't want it," he stated lamely. "I thought maybe your son would like it."

"Oh, I'm sure he would," she replied, assessing the bicycle with a dubious expression.

"It's what I prayed for, right, Mama?"

"Yes," she answered slowly, "it seems to fit your exact description."

"I prayed for a red-and-black mountain bike," Tyler told Alec, fairly gyrating in all his excitement.

"Well, here you go." Alec lifted the thing over the fence. "It's all yours."

"We can't accept such a gift—"

"Really, you'd be doing me a favor. It's way too small a bike for me anyway. I'd just have to find another way to get rid of it. And after all, it is the answer to the boy's prayer."

Lydia smiled. "That's very generous of you, Mr. . .?"

"Corbett. Alec Corbett. Call me Alec." He wanted to bite off his tongue for rambling on like such an idiot!

She smiled. "Well. . .Alec. . .you're very generous. Thank you."

"Aw, it's nothing. Like I said, I bought it for someone who didn't want it."

Tyler straddled the bike. It looked a little big for him, although he managed to reach the pedals from the seat. He took a quick, but shaky spin around the wide end of the driveway.

"Let me grab my tools and then you bring that bike over here," Alec told the boy. "Maybe I can lower the seat a notch—the handlebars, too."

"Thanks!" Tyler beamed, while Brooke had gone back to her swing, watching the scene from afar. He glanced at his mother. "Can I?"

She hesitated, then nodded. "Yes, but don't make a pest of yourself. I'm sure our new neighbor has a lot of other things to accomplish today."

"Naw, nothing's going on. It's okay," Alec heard himself say before he winced inwardly. He had a kazillion things to do! Something about this modern-day Southern belle caused him to act as though he didn't have a brain in his head!

"Now God just has to answer my other prayer. . .for a new daddy. I don't suppose you can help Him out with that one, too, Mr. Alec."

"Tyler!" his mother declared, a crimson blush running up her neck and cheeks.

Alec grinned sardonically, his senses returning in full force. "Sorry, pal," he said, gazing at Tyler's innocent countenance. "God's on His own, there."

He glanced at Lydia, who wore an expression of chagrin. She seemed sincere, but then Denise had seemed sincere, too—at first. Was it a mask? Maybe Lydia Boswick coaxed her kids to "break the ice" with eligible men. Maybe she played the same kind of games that all women played. Well, he wouldn't fall for it again. Praying for a husband, was she? Well, it wouldn't be him!

"Nice meeting you," he said curtly, adding a stiff nod before turning and striding toward his house. No way was he going to get sucked in by another female's wiles. Not even if she was a pretty little thing with kitten-gray eyes who looked as though she'd welcome the strength of a man.

Right.

He unlocked his back door and walked into the hallway. Women like Lydia Boswick could appeal to a male's ego, that's for sure! But he wasn't going to be swayed by her Southern charm. No sir. Not him!

three

"Tyler, you shouldn't have said that!"

"Said what?"

Lydia gazed into her eight-year-old's face, noting his dark brown eyes were veiled with naiveté. "Oh, never mind," she replied gently, unable to reprimand her son right there and then. They'd have to discuss proper social etiquette another time. "Just make sure you don't go inside the neighbor's house, all right?"

"Why, Mama?"

"Because we don't know Mr. Corbett very well, now do we? Besides, I'm sure he has plenty to do since he just moved in yesterday."

"Okay. . ."

Lydia turned toward the house as Tyler led his new bicycle down the driveway. She entered the kitchen and spotted her straight-backed mother-in-law, standing at the sink, cleaning up lunch dishes.

"Who's that man you were conversing with, Lydia?" she asked over one narrow shoulder.

"My new neighbor. He just moved in yesterday and would you believe he gave Tyler a bicycle? Why, it looks brand new!"

Elberta Boswick turned off the faucet and swung around. "He gave that boy a bicycle?" Her face was heavily lined with age and even more so now that she was frowning. "And you allowed it?"

Lydia shifted uncomfortably. "Yes, Elberta. I mean, I didn't see a reason to reject the kind offer. And Tyler so wanted a bike just exactly like it. . . ."

"We Boswicks take care of our own, Lydia," she stated sharply. "You know that. If Tyler had a need, you should have

23

let Gerald know about it."

Lydia opened her mouth to explain herself, but thought better of it. Elberta was a proud woman and often looked at gifts as charity—something the Boswicks would never stoop to accept. Why, they'd starve to death first! Hadn't their ancestors done much the same during the Civil War? Ah, yes, Lydia had heard all about it and, generally, she felt privileged to have a part in such a wealth of heritage. Unfortunately, her mother-in-law had never treated her with the same kindnesses as a *real* member of the Boswick family. It used to anger Michael, but it hurt Lydia. Still did.

"What's going on here?" Gerald Boswick asked curiously, entering the kitchen, a cup and saucer in his right hand. A tall man, pushing sixty years old, he remained a handsome and imposing figure. Lydia had always thought he resembled the Hollywood actor Kirk Douglas, right down to the cleft in his chin.

"Lydia," Elberta ground out, turning back to the sink, "has allowed Tyler to accept a bicycle from a perfect stranger."

Gerald glanced at Lydia, sending her an affectionate wink—one that said he'd handle his wife just as he always did.

"Well now, dear, I won't have you fretting over a bike. I'll take care of everything. Lydia and I will have a talk later."

"Good."

Lydia exchanged a glance with her father-in-law, knowing he'd allow Tyler to keep the bike. Gerald denied the children and her nothing. In fact, Lydia didn't know what she would have done if her father-in-law hadn't stepped in after Michael died. She'd been so frightened, worried, and dazed—with Michael gone, Lydia had felt helpless.

That was when Gerald efficiently took over, handling everything from funeral and burial arrangements to insurance policies and bank statements. Then he'd suggested she become his secretary at SPCC. He promised her flexible hours so Tyler and Brooke would never have to be in daycare. He said it would keep her mind off her grief and he'd been right. Moreover, he took on the role of her agent, paying her monthly bills and mortgage payment, drawing out of the funds from Michael's life insurance policy, and Lydia felt indebted to Gerald Boswick for his unfailing care and protection.

"How about some more coffee, dear?" he asked now with a winning smile that caused his dark eyes to dance.

"Yes, of course. . ."

She crossed the room, took his cup, then strode to the counter by the sink, where the pot of flavored brew sat warming in its automatic maker. As she reached for the carafe, she glanced out the window and spied Tyler watching Mr. Alec Corbett at work on the bicycle. She poured the coffee, eyeing her new neighbor speculatively. He'd removed his tie and navy suit jacket, revealing a white dress shirt tucked into dark blue pants. *He is quite a handsome man*, she admitted inwardly, taking another note of his full head of sandy-blond hair. He had an athletic look about him, and she guessed him to be an inch or two taller than her father-in-law, who stood over six feet. And such broad shoulders, muscular arms—

"Lydia!"

At Elberta's shriek, Lydia stopped pouring the coffee, realizing she'd overfilled the cup and now the steaming liquid was spilling onto the counter.

"Good heavens, what's the matter with you?" Elberta asked, rag in hand ready to wipe up the mess.

Lydia felt a blush warming her cheeks. "I was. . .um. . .just watching Tyler," she fibbed. Then, silently, she had to ask herself the same question: What *was* the matter with her? She wasn't one to gawk at strange men.

Cleaning off the saucer, she turned to Gerald and handed him his coffee. "I'm so sorry," she murmured, feeling oddly nervous. "Forgive me."

He narrowed his gaze suspiciously. "Quite all right, my dear. No harm done."

꒰ꕤ꒱

Alec attended church that evening and, afterward, grabbed a

quick hamburger with a couple of new friends. He got home near nine o'clock.

Inside his house, he pulled off his tie, tossed his jacket onto the nearest chair, and gazed around the living room at the myriad of cardboard boxes waiting to be unpacked. Why had he played around with a bike and an eight-year-old this afternoon instead of setting up housekeeping?

He collapsed into his burgundy leather-upholstered couch, recalling the conversation he'd had with Tyler.

"Do you think my mama is pretty?" the boy had asked, throwing Alec momentarily off guard.

"Well," he hedged, not wanting to lie, but careful to show his disinterest, "she is, as far as women go, I guess."

"She is. . .pretty?"

"I guess."

Tyler had grinned broadly. "So, you think my mama is pretty, huh?"

Alec straightened. "Get on that bike, kid," he'd said gruffly, "and let me see if it fits you better."

"Yes, sir."

The lowered handlebars and seat seemed to make things easier for Tyler, and Alec had watched the boy ride down his driveway, into the street, and around to his own backyard.

That was when Tyler's grandfather emerged from the house.

"Welcome to Woodruff," the older man said, striding confidently to the fence.

Alec met him, regarding his expensive, smartly tailored dark suit. They shook hands, and Alec introduced himself.

"And I'm Gerald Boswick, the pastor at Southern Pride Community Church."

"Good to meet you."

The older man puffed out his chest and stuck his hands in his pants pockets. "So, what line of work are you in, Alex?"

"Alec," he'd corrected, although he got the distinct impression Pastor Boswick had purposely mispronounced his name. "I'm a carpenter."

"You don't say? Well, that's interesting. . .hammering furniture together, eh? Prefab stuff, I imagine. Everything is prefab these days."

The pastor was wrong. Alec was a craftsman, but he held his tongue. He'd lived long enough to know some people really didn't care what a guy did for a living. They were either just trying to start conversation or they liked to hear themselves talk. The latter, Alec guessed, was probably the case in this situation.

"So, how'd you get into that line of work?"

"Always liked woodworking in high school," he'd replied with a shrug. "After I graduated, I attended a tech school and went on for my apprenticeship, and. . . ," Alec shrugged once more, "here I am."

"And here you are," Pastor Boswick drawled in repetition as his mouth curved upward in a wry grin. "Tyler tells me you're from up north."

"Yep." Alec smiled. "I'm a Yankee and proud of it."

"Well," Pastor Boswick had replied with a curt, but amused chuckle, "I wouldn't go advertising that fact, if I were you. There're still folks here in Woodruff who haven't quite gotten over their bad feelings for Northerners."

"A one hundred and forty year grudge, huh?"

"Guess you could say that."

"And are you one of those 'folks' with a chip on your shoulder?" Alec had asked, unable to keep the challenge out of his voice.

"Of course not. Everyone's equal in the sight of God. But you'd be wise to heed my warning, son, just the same. . . ."

His warning, Alec thought cynically, rising from the couch now. There was something about the good pastor that really bothered him. Perhaps it was his air of superiority. Nevertheless, Alec hadn't encountered any trouble in town. So far he'd been well-received, despite the fact he was a *Northerner*.

Walking down the beige-carpeted hallway of his single-story home, Alec entered his bedroom and changed clothes.

Unable to help himself, he pulled on his favorite Wisconsin Badgers sweatshirt, thinking, *You can take the Yankee out of the North, but you can't take the North out of the Yankee. . . . Just what am I doing in North Carolina anyway?*

Regardless of the momentary doubt, Alec knew the answer to that question. He'd moved here to start a new life, and so far, so good. New job, new house. . .

The doorbell chimed and he peered out the front door's half-moon-shaped window before answering it. "And a new neighbor," he muttered, before greeting Lydia with a stiff smile.

"Well, Mrs. Boswick, what a surprise," Alec said, flicking on the porch light.

"Sorry to bother you," she stated sweetly. Alec wondered if her amiable demeanor was part of her act—her scheme to get a husband. "Our bathroom sink is clogged something awful and I wondered if you might have a pliers so I can take off the pipe."

"A pliers?" Alec tried not to snicker. "Personally, I'd use a wrench to take off a pipe."

"Oh. . .well, that's what I meant. Excuse me." Lydia smiled. "I'm not very familiar with tools. I usually call my father-in-law when I need help, but I can't locate either of my in-laws right now. And my neighbors on the other side, Connie and Terrence Wilberson. . .well, they're out of town, visiting one of Connie's relatives, and—"

"Look, I've got a wrench, and you can borrow it," Alec interrupted, "but, um. . ." He raised a brow. "Are you sure you'd know what to do with it?"

She lifted her chin defiantly. "Yes. I'm quite capable, thank you."

"Okay. I'll go get it for you. Want to come in?" He opened the screen door, bidding her entrance.

"No," she replied, shaking her head. "I don't believe that'd be proper. I'll wait right here. Besides, I don't like to leave my children unattended, and they're both standing right up there in that window." Turning slightly, she pointed toward her red brick home. "There they are. . .right where I can see them."

She waved and Alec stepped onto the porch so he could see if what she said was true. Sure enough, Tyler and Brooke stood at the window where the white mini blinds had been pulled up. When the children saw him, they smiled and waved vigorously.

Alec grinned and glanced at Lydia. "Be right back with the wrench."

"Thank you," she said demurely.

As he walked through the living room, dining area, and into the kitchen where his tools lay already unpacked but awaiting their permanent place in his home, Alec felt a pang of obligation. He supposed he should help the lady, seeing as he knew a little something about plumbing while it didn't sound like she was even sure how to use a wrench. Besides, if she really meant to work her female wiles on him, she'd have accepted his invitation and entered his house, yet she preferred to wait outside where the temperatures had plummeted into the forties—for propriety's sake, she'd said. Somehow, her decision gave Alec pause. Maybe he'd been wrong about her, but he still wasn't entirely convinced.

Toolbox in hand, he strode back through the house, stepping out onto the porch. Lydia took one look at the large, red, metal container he carried and cast him a nervous smile.

"You know, I was just thinking maybe I'd call one of those emergency plumbing places."

"On a Sunday? At this hour?" Alec shook his head. "They'll charge you a fortune."

"But, I'm not sure if I can—"

"Carry this heavy toolbox over to your place, much less use a wrench?" He chuckled softly. "Yeah, I figured. How 'bout I come over and see what I can do instead?"

An expression of relief flittered across her delicate features, softly illuminated by the porch light. "That's very kind of you. . .thanks."

Lydia led the way down the steps, over the lawn, and to her house. Alec had admired the structure from afar yesterday while he moved in, and it was every bit as impressive on the inside as he'd imagined—perhaps even more so.

He gazed appreciatively at the mahogany woodwork in her living room, noting the built-in bookcases on either side of the fireplace on the far wall. Next he marveled at the beautiful banister and railing as he walked up the polished wooden stairs.

"This is some house you've got here."

"Why, thank you. I'm partial to it." Lydia paused on the first landing. "When my husband, Michael, and I first looked at this house, he said it was haunted because of its poor condition. And I must say, it appeared that way, broken shutters outside banging against the house in the wind, peeling paint, rotting wood and spider webs galore inside! The kitchen was a ghastly sight, terribly outdated. The two bathrooms, one downstairs and this one up here, were equally as obsolete. But I managed to talk Michael into buying it anyway. I just imagined what this house would look like once it had been restored." She gave him a bittersweet smile. "I'm glad my husband had shared my vision. We had a lot of good times fixing up this old place."

Alec merely nodded, feeling fascinated. "Did you do the refurbishing yourself?"

"Yes, most of it anyway."

She turned and he followed her the rest of the way upstairs, where the kids met them in the hallway. After a grand welcome, Lydia instructed Tyler and Brooke to go to their bedrooms and read until she and "Mr. Alec" finished up with the clogged sink.

"So you can remodel a home, but can't use a wrench, eh?" he asked half-teasingly.

"I can paint and I can wallpaper, if that's what you mean. But when it comes to nuts and bolts, I'm lost. And plumbing. . .? Forget it, although I was willing to give it a try tonight."

Assessing the situation, Alec concluded that the sink had

overflowed, judging by the water still in its basin and the heap of wet towels in the bathtub.

Lydia stepped back and watched him expertly take the pipes apart.

"Would you mind stopping the drain so I don't get soaked?"

She did as he asked, having to step over his long, horizontal form in the process. Minutes later, Alec had disconnected the U-shaped pipe from the drain.

"Got a wire hanger?"

"Yes." Lydia ran to fetch the object, and when she returned, he straightened it out and stuck it into the pipe, producing a glob of unsightly hair and unidentifiable muck. Then he poked and prodded and, much to Lydia's surprise, a small, die-cast metal car fell into his outstretched palm.

"I think this has been in here for a while," he said amusedly, inspecting the rusty thing. "You might ask Ty about it."

Alec chuckled and tossed the slimy toy at her. Lydia grimaced, but caught it while he began replacing the piping. Once it was secure again, he stood and pulled the sink's stopper. The water went down easily.

"Thank you," Lydia said gratefully.

"No sweat. That was an easy one."

He washed his hands, dried them, picked up his tools, and then strode into the hallway, where Lydia was waiting. "G'night, you two," he called toward Tyler and Brooke's bedrooms.

They rushed out to say good-bye and marveled at how fast he'd fixed the clogged drain. Lydia rolled her eyes, somewhat embarrassed that her children were treating the man like a superhero.

"All right, back to bed," she ordered. "I'm going to see Mr. Alec out and then I'll be up to hear your prayers."

"You got some polite kids there, Mrs. Boswick, I'll grant you that much."

"Why, thank you." It wasn't the first time she'd heard the compliment, and Lydia felt very proud of her children.

"But let me say this," Alec began, pivoting just before he reached the front door. "I was just being neighborly tonight. Doing the Christian thing, nothing else. Got it?"

"You're saying that because of what Tyler said this morning, aren't you?" Lydia asked perceptively. "Well, to be honest, I'm not shopping for a daddy for my children, if that's what you think." Her voice was calm and steady. "I surely can't blame you for being put off but, you see, children often speak their minds without thinking first. I am truly sorry if you were offended."

"Yeah, well, I—"

"The truth is, I don't want to remarry. I loved my husband so much and. . .well, I just don't think I could ever feel that way about anyone ever again."

She yanked on the heavy, polished front door and it opened. Alec stepped out of the house and onto her two-story covered front porch.

"Thank you for your help tonight."

"Sure thing."

"Good night, Mr. Corbett."

"Alec," he reminded her as the large front door closed in his face.

Slowly, he made his way back to his house. When he arrived, he cast one last glance at the Boswick place across the way. Why did he suddenly feel as though that woman with her sweet, Southern manner was a challenge he'd like to accept?

Forget her, you fool, he groused inwardly. *She's not looking for a romantic relationship and neither are you. So just forget her!*

four

Once his wife entered the bathroom and busied herself with her nightly routine, Gerald Boswick lifted the phone, dialing the number he'd come to know so well. With the receiver to his ear, he listened as it rang while he tapped the toe of his shoe impatiently. After a few moments, he seated himself on the wide bed covered with a pale blue satin comforter and allowed his gaze to take in the opulent splendor of the rest of the room. Elberta had hired just the right decorator—a darling little thing from Nashville. What was her name again?

The phone suddenly stopped ringing. "It's me," he said, announcing himself.

"What can I do for you on this late Sunday night?"

"I think you'd better step up the romance," Gerald advised.

"I thought you told me to take it slow."

"Things have changed."

A pause. "What things?"

"She's got a new neighbor. I met him this afternoon and if we're not careful, he could ruin everything."

"What do you suggest?"

"I'll make some arrangements; you just do your part. Woo and coo her as though your life depends on it." Gerald paused for effect, the way he'd been taught back in seminary training. "Because it does."

❧

On Monday morning, Lydia deposited Tyler and Brooke in their respective classrooms at Southern Pride Christian School before making her way around the large building to where the church office suites were located. They consisted of three offices: her father-in-law's, the assistant pastor's, and the youth pastor's. Lydia's desk was centered between them, as she did

some secretarial work for all three men. However, the majority
of her time was spent answering calls and scheduling appoint-
ments for Gerald, as well as tending to minor bookkeeping
responsibilities. Once inside her warm, violet-carpeted work
space, she made a pot of coffee and set it in the reception area.
As usual, her father-in-law had one appointment after another
today.

As she walked to her desk, adjacent to the small lobby,
Lydia noticed the Do Not Disturb sign on Gerald's office door
and heard voices coming from within. A female's—her father-
in-law's. She glanced at her wristwatch. Odd, she thought. It
was only eight o'clock. Lydia did all the scheduling and she
never penciled anything in before nine. But perhaps a crisis
arose, so he'd created the slot himself.

She sat down and momentarily glanced at the row of pictures on the back of her desktop. Tyler, Brooke, Michael, and
herself. Her family, minus one, and in spite of what she'd told
her neighbor last night, the loss of her husband had left a
chasm in her heart that ached to be filled. Except she seriously doubted she'd ever love again, that she could find the
kind of soul mate she'd found in Michael.

The outer door suddenly opened, bringing Lydia out of her
lonesome reverie, and a lovely African-American woman
stepped into the reception area. She wore a tan rain-or-shine
coat and had a large leather satchel draped over her left shoulder. In her other arm, she carried a day planner.

"May I help you?" Lydia asked politely, rising slowly from
her chair.

"Yes." The woman came forward and set her planner on the
desk. "I'm Michelle Marx from the *Charlotte Observer.*"

"A reporter?" Lydia asked, surprised.

"That's right. I wanted to know if I could speak with Pastor
Boswick regarding allegations that were made by some of his
former church members. Is he in?"

"Allegations?"

"Yes. You're not aware of them?"

"Um, no. . ."

At that very moment, the door to Gerald's office swung open and he stepped out, followed by an attractive blond named Cindy Tanner. Lydia knew Cindy and her husband were having awful marital problems. The man had left her and their two young children, and Cindy was heartbroken, so she consulted with Gerald frequently.

"Thank you, Pastor," she murmured with a grateful expression. "I don't know what I'd do without you."

"There, now, Cindy, you're going to be fine. A good shepherd always takes care of his flock and, as I said, I will take care of you."

Lydia felt a moment's pride at how chivalrous her father-in-law sounded in front of the reporter wanting to investigate him. But the way Cindy gazed up adoringly at him caused Lydia a good measure of discomfort. Was that a come-hither look? Lydia glanced at Gerald. Was he looking back? Lydia checked herself. Of course he wasn't flirting. How could she have even thought such a thing?

She cleared her throat. Both the pastor and Cindy turned toward her.

"Pastor Boswick," Lydia began formally since they were in the workplace, "this is Michelle Marx. She's a reporter."

"How do you do, Pastor," Michelle replied with a tight smile.

He nodded curtly, then whispered something to Cindy, who turned and left the office. After watching her go, he wheeled his gaze back to the journalist and assessed her in two sweeping glances. "I don't have time for reporters," he stated at last. "Have a good day." With that, he turned and headed for his office.

"But. . ." Lydia's argument was lost on the oak-paneled door that closed soundly behind him.

"Not very friendly for a pastor," Michelle remarked.

Lydia fingered her phone and thought about buzzing him but noticed his line was lit; he was already on his extension.

She glanced at the visitor. "I'm sorry, Ms. Marx."

The woman shrugged. "I'll just have to print the story with what I've got. But I can promise you, it won't be pretty."

Lydia felt a moment's panic. "Perhaps I should try to talk him into speaking with you. Just a moment." She made for Gerald's office, but Michelle halted her.

"Don't bother. I think I've seen and heard enough."

"No, wait. . ."

Lydia glanced at her father-in-law's door, wondering why he was behaving so brusquely this morning. That wasn't like him. Turning, she followed Michelle into the outer hallway, unable to abide the thought of the woman slandering the Boswick name.

"Perhaps I can help," she called after the reporter who stopped in midstride. "Please, come back into the office. I'll get you some coffee and we can talk."

Pivoting, the woman eyed her speculatively.

"I'm Lydia Boswick, the pastor's daughter-in-law, and. . . well, since I work here, I might be able to answer some of your questions."

One well-sculptured eyebrow went up. "His daughter-in-law, huh? Yes, all right. . ."

Back inside the reception area, Lydia poured coffee and then sat down in one of the lilac-printed upholstered armchairs. "Now, what allegations were you referring to, Ms. Marx?"

She flipped open her planner. "Do you know who Jordan and Sherry Smith are?"

"Why, yes," Lydia replied with a curious frown. Sherry had once been Lydia's best friend.

"Mr. Smith was the treasurer here, wasn't he?"

"Yes."

"Hmm. . .well, according to Mr. Smith, Pastor Boswick uses some unethical, if not illegal, practices to ensure the church's financial stability as well as his own. He says that was why he left Southern Pride Community Church. Is that true?"

Lydia tried to hide her surprise. Unethical? Her father-in-law? "Not to my knowledge. I understood the Smiths left SPCC for entirely different reasons."

"I see. And what about Mrs. Belva Applegate and Miss Marion Campbell? Their families plan to file lawsuits, but the district attorney's office states that it plans to file its own charges of extortion against the pastor some time this week. Can you tell me about this?"

"Extortion?" This time Lydia couldn't conceal her shock.

"You don't know? The families claim Pastor Boswick used undue influence to convince the two elderly women to purchase expensive term life insurance policies, naming him as beneficiary instead of paying for necessary medical treatments. The result, the families allege, was the premature deaths of their loved ones."

"I don't believe that's the case at all," Lydia replied, raising her chin defensively. "Both Mrs. Applegate and Miss Campbell were elderly women who were quite sickly much of the time."

"So you don't believe medical care from a licensed provider might have forestalled their deaths?"

"Neither woman wanted to go into a nursing home, so many of us here at church took turns preparing meals, cleaning, writing letters—"

"You, personally, helped care for the women?"

"I took my turn, yes. Once a month. And they were lovely gentlewomen who were grateful to be in their own homes at the end of their lives."

"Hmm. . ." The reporter nodded thoughtfully. "Well, is it true that many more women are accepted into the fold here at Southern Pride Community Church than are men?"

"I beg your pardon?"

"Especially widows and single women?"

Lydia frowned. "I don't know. I guess I never noticed anything like that." She shifted uncomfortably, recalling that her own mother had been a widow when they had first come to SPCC, back when Lydia was sixteen years old. But so what?

"Is it true that scores of men are turned away from this church every year because Pastor Boswick will not abide anyone disagreeing with his theology?"

"No, that's not true," Lydia answered confidently. "Many of our members are high-profile men in the community."

She smiled weakly, but Michelle's expression remained stony. "Do they agree with your father-in-law on every issue?"

"Probably not."

"But you're not sure?"

Lydia swallowed hard, thinking that the woman missed her calling as a lawyer. Why, she was as good at interrogating a subject as Michael had been!

Then suddenly her smile broadened. "Yes, I'm sure. My husband didn't agree with his father on every issue. He was very opinionated and they debated quite often." Lydia sat back in the chair. "So you see, that's a misconception."

"I noticed that you speak of your husband in the past tense."

"He died two and a half years ago."

"How unfortunate. I'm sorry."

Glancing down at her hands folded neatly in her lap, Lydia merely nodded.

"And what about Patricia Reimer Jackson. Do you know her?"

Lydia raised her head quickly. "Yes." She swallowed the fact that Patricia Jackson was her mother.

"Is it true Mrs. Jackson was church disciplined for rebellion simply because she was a widow who wanted to marry a man who was not a member of Southern Pride Community Church?"

"There's a little more to it than that."

"Oh? What more?" Michelle took up her pen, ready to write down anything Lydia might say.

But she didn't utter a sound. How could she? It'd been a horrible, shameful situation.

"Was Mrs. Jackson openly rebellious?"

"Yes," Lydia forced herself to reply.

"She was rebellious because she wanted to remarry and Pastor Boswick was against the match?"

"Yes."

"So, going against Pastor Boswick's will is open rebellion and grounds for church discipline here at Southern Pride Community Church. Is that correct?"

"That's a blanket statement and I can't possibly answer a simple 'yes' or 'no.' "

"I see. . ."

"Are you insinuating my father-in-law is a legalistic man?"

"Isn't he? From the reports I've heard—"

"No!" Lydia raised her chin. "He maintains high standards, but he's not legalistic."

Michelle put the capped end of the pen against her lower lip thoughtfully. "Back to Mrs. Jackson. . .she stated she discovered after she was disciplined by the church that Pastor Boswick had years ago coerced her into signing over her late husband's life insurance funds while she'd been under the impression he was merely managing them for her. Do you know anything about that?"

"It wasn't coercion. My. . .Mrs. Jackson," she said, catching herself, "donated those funds to SPCC."

Lydia still remembered the night her mother had signed the documents. Michael had come along and they'd sat together on the sofa, where they talked and he comforted her in her grief over losing her dad. That was really when it all began— they fell in love while business matters were being settled in the dining room.

"So, Mrs. Jackson donated the funds and Pastor Boswick promised her security and safety within the arms of Southern Pride Community Church. But once she was no longer a member, she no longer had that protection—or her money. Is that right?"

"Well, sort of. . .Pastor Boswick can only offer protection to his flock."

"But he can keep the flock's money regardless."

"It was a donation," Lydia maintained. She stood, suddenly desiring to end the cross-examination. "I have work to do, Ms. Marx, and I think you should be on your way."

"I understand, but answer me one more question," Michelle said, standing and looping her bag over her shoulder. "Is it true that Southern Pride Community Church's membership is all white? No African Americans? No Hispanics? No Hmong or Native Americans?"

"Um. . ." Lydia had to think. Weren't there other races represented here? SPCC was a large church and drew people from within a thirty-mile radius around Woodruff, Gastonia, and Charlotte—surely it was racially blended. "I'm afraid I honestly don't know the answer to your question, Ms. Marx," she replied lamely.

"Well," she said, throwing Lydia a disappointed look, "thanks for your time, anyway."

"You're not still going to print the article about those allegations against my father-in-law, are you?"

"You better believe I am!" The journalist turned and strode toward the door. "My readers deserve to know the truth, and I hope to bring it to light. Have a nice day, Mrs. Boswick."

Lydia stared in horror after the woman. The truth? She couldn't possibly know the truth! Her father-in-law was the kindest, most caring man on earth, not some criminal!

The phone rang, and Lydia snapped to her senses, walked back to her desk, and answered it. It was the assistant pastor's wife, Eileen Camden.

"I haven't seen him this morning, but I can put you through to his voice mail."

"Sure, that would be fine. Thanks."

She took care of the call just as Gerald reappeared from his office. "That woman," she said with jangled nerves, "that reporter—"

"I hope you got rid of her."

Lydia swallowed. "She left. But she promised to print some

awful lies about you."

Her father-in-law puffed out his chest and grinned wryly. "Lydia, my dear, the Lord said there would be persecution from the world when we try to further God's kingdom. I'm not afraid of anything the newspapers might disclose. Such things have happened to me before. Every intelligent person knows those daily newspapers are filled with gossip and sensationalism."

"Yes, of course. Everyone knows that—"

"Don't let it upset you. Now, what about my coffee?"

Lydia managed a smile. "Coming right up."

✺

As much as Lydia tried to take Gerald's advice, she felt anxious for the rest of the day. The questions Michelle Marx had asked troubled her and put doubts into her head, causing her to feel confused. But, as her father-in-law often said from the pulpit, questions were the workings of the devil. After all, Satan had questioned Eve in the garden, causing her to doubt God's word. . . .

By early afternoon, Lydia determined to push aside her worry and concentrate on her work. The hours ticked by. Soon it was three-thirty and Tyler and Brooke burst into the church offices.

"Hi, Mama. Ready to go home?" Tyler asked in his usual exuberant tone.

"Lower your voice, Ty," Lydia lightly scolded him. "And I'm just about done."

"Well, well, two of my favorite people," Gerald said, strolling out from his quarters. "I thought I heard you come in, Tyler."

Lydia grinned. Tyler with his boisterous ways could be heard for a mile. Gerald liked to say he was "a preacher in the making."

"And, little Brooke. . .you just get prettier every day."

"Thank you, Grampa," she said, beaming.

While the children chattered amicably with their grandfather, Lydia cleared her desk and prepared to leave. Then

Gerald scooted them into the outer hallway, motioning with his head for Lydia to join him in his office.

"What is it?" Lydia asked, trailing him. She felt certain he'd bring up the reporter. But to her surprise, such was not the case.

"Simeon Crenshaw phoned earlier, saying he needs an escort to a dinner meeting this evening. He asked my permission to take you, and I told him you'd be delighted to go along."

Lydia frowned. "But—"

"Elberta and I will take the children overnight. I'll follow you home, you can pack their things and still have plenty of time to pretty yourself up for your date."

"Gerald, I don't want to go out with Sim Crenshaw. I'm not interested in him."

"Now, Lydia, Sim is a brother in Christ, an upstanding member here at SPCC, and he's my attorney. Furthermore, you and I agreed that I'd have the say on whom you dated. That way, you won't feel pressured to accept or turn away a possible suitor. I've suggested Sim before, but this time, you'll go out with him, all right?"

Gerald gave her an indulgent smile. "Women are so emotional, as you well know. And so vulnerable. The weaker vessel."

Lydia managed a nod. That was what the Bible said: the weaker vessel. And since Michael died, she'd been emotionally shipwrecked. She had come to depend on her father-in-law's guidance and protection. She needed him.

"You need me. Am I right?" he asked as if divining her thoughts.

"Yes."

"Good. Then you're willing to continue with our arrangement. I'd like to see you remarry. . .go on with your life."

"I'm trying," she insisted.

"You need a husband," Gerald maintained. "Someone who can take a firm hand to Tyler and set a good example for him. That boy is the apple of my eye, you know." A faraway look entered his swarthy gaze. "He's all I have left, since Michael died. . . ."

Lydia sensed that Gerald still missed his son deeply, just as she did at times. Nevertheless, she just couldn't enter into a marital relationship that was not of her choosing. "Gerald, Simeon Crenshaw is not the man for me, nor is he the kind of father I'd want for my children."

"You say that now, dear, but that's because you haven't gotten to know Sim. He can really be quite charming. You'll see."

"But, I—"

"Lydia, dear, won't you please go out with him tonight as a special favor to me? I'm going to require Sim's help in the next few months, what with all these horrible accusations stacked against me." Lowering his voice, he smiled. "Couldn't you just help me get on his good side?"

"You're already on his good side," she assured him.

Gerald's gaze hardened in a way that caused Lydia to retreat from further debate. She didn't want to go out with Sim, but more than anything, she wanted to please her father-in-law. Her own father had died when she was seven years old, and Gerald Boswick was the only father-figure she'd ever known. He'd been generous and compassionate to her, despite his wife's subtle animosity—and in spite of her mother's rebellion—and he'd helped Lydia over the most difficult time in her life when Michael died. How, then, could she let Gerald down after all he'd done for her over the years?

"Yes, I'll go out with Simeon Crenshaw tonight," she forced herself to reply, albeit reluctantly.

"Wonderful. He'll be delighted." Pulling her into a quick embrace, her father-in-law kissed her cheek. "That's my girl. Chin up. Smile. That's it. Now, let me get my car keys, and we'll call it a day."

Nodding, Lydia fetched her purse and coat. *Oh, Lord,* she silently pleaded, *help me make it through this night.*

five

Settling himself into a white plastic lawn chair on the front porch, Alec stretched out lazily. The weather had been mild today—another seventy-degree day. Some of the guys at work said the annual spring rain showers would begin soon and suggested Alec enjoy the sun while he could. So now, as the fiery red ball began its descent in the western sky, he reveled in its fading glory.

After a few minutes passed, he glanced next door, thinking it had been awfully quiet over at the Boswick house this evening. He guessed they were home, since the family mini-van was parked in the driveway. He shrugged and lifted his newspaper. Maybe the kids had to stay inside and do their homework. In any case, it wasn't any of his concern.

Leafing through the newspaper, Alec scanned the headlines until one in particular caught his attention. *Local Pastor to Face Extortion Charges.* Interested, he read on, nearly choking on the first sentence. *Gerald Boswick, pastor of Southern Pride Community Church, is likely to be formally charged with extortion later this week, according to the district attorney's office.*

Alec let out a long, slow whistle, casting another glance next door. Perhaps that was why it had been so quiet over there.

As soon as he'd completed the thought, a silver Lincoln Continental pulled into Lydia's driveway. Alec watched curiously as a short, stocky man with dark brown, woolly hair climbed out of the driver's side and walked up to the front door. Within moments, Lydia emerged from the house, wearing a black silk dress with burgundy trim and a matching jacket. Her chestnut brown hair was swept up, regally, emphasizing her delicate features and, even from his distance, Alec noticed her wide, but nicely shaped lips, painted the same color as the trim of her dress.

Alec felt his jaw drop in awe, but quickly snapped it shut. But there was no doubt about it: Lydia Boswick was gorgeous! Was she going on a date with that fuzzy little elf in the navy pinstriped suit?

Good thing she's got better taste in homes than in men, Alec thought dryly, *or else I'd be living next door to a major eyesore!*

Watching her gracefully stroll toward the Lincoln, Alec folded his newspaper, catching her attention. Lydia smiled a brief greeting, but something in her gaze told him she wasn't very happy. Either the nasty business surrounding her father-in-law troubled her, or she wasn't very excited about going on this date, he decided. And as the car backed out of the Boswicks' driveway, Alec found himself wishing the latter were the cause of her discontent.

Knucklehead, he chided himself, reopening the newspaper. *There could be a million reasons why Lydia doesn't seem happy. Maybe she's not even going on a date. Maybe she's going to a funeral. That'd make anyone look somber!*

In any case, Alec found himself having a difficult time dismissing his pretty neighbor from his thoughts.

❧

Alec dozed, only to awaken suddenly to the sound of a car door slamming. Then another. He roused himself, feeling a stiffness in his back and, lifting his feet from the wide brick porch rail, he wriggled his toes, trying to get the circulation back into them. He'd fallen asleep right there in the lawn chair! At that very moment Lydia and her date walked up the driveway.

"How about I come in for a while and make us both some cappuccino?" her escort suggested. "Chocolate? French vanilla?"

Lydia stopped short. "Not tonight. I'm very tired."

Alec grinned. Yeah, he'd heard that excuse before.

He sat very still in the darkness, waiting for Lydia to move again so he could get up and go into the house undetected. As it was, he felt as though he were watching a play since the spotlight from Lydia's porch streamed down on her and the fuzzy-haired guy trying to persuade her not to end their date. But Alec didn't want to appear the spying neighbor and if he stood right then, they'd know he'd been there and likely be embarrassed—and so would he.

"Well, then, how about a good-night kiss, Lydia?"

Alec groaned inwardly. This was getting worse by the moment.

"Why, Sim," Lydia drawled politely, "I'm flattered you asked, but I never kiss on the first date."

Alec held his breath, trying not to laugh out loud. Sim? What kind of name was that for a human being? And get a load of that expression; he obviously didn't appreciate being turned down.

Lydia turned to climb the steps of her porch, but Sim caught her arm.

"Just a little kiss? Please?"

She jerked out of his grasp, looking surprised. "No."

"But I've waited all night to kiss you. I've waited months to kiss you. . .years, even!"

"Sim!" She stepped backwards, and he grabbed her shoulders.

"Just one kiss. . ."

"No! Stop it!"

Although her voice wasn't loud, Alec could hear the note of desperation and something inside him snapped into action. He stood and found himself over on Lydia's driveway before he even realized what he was doing there. Taking hold of the elf by the back of his shirt collar, Alec yanked him away from Lydia.

"I believe the lady wants you to back off."

Astonishment flashed across the shorter man's face, but it

quickly turned to contempt. "Who are you? Mind your own business!"

Alec didn't reply, but turned to Lydia as he released the man from his grasp. She appeared shaken, but unharmed. "You're free to go inside if you like," he said calmly.

She nodded and, after tossing the other man a look of mild disdain, she hurried up the steps to the porch, unlocked her front door, and disappeared into the house.

When Alec glanced back at Sim, he was already heading toward his Lincoln, muttering under his breath. He got in, closed the door, and pealed out of the driveway.

"Hey, little man," Alec said as if the guy could hear him, "you're doing it all wrong. You've got to sweet talk a woman into a good-night kiss, not act like an ogre."

Shaking his head, Alec watched the car take off down the dimly lit street, wondering if he'd be able to get a good-night kiss out of Lydia Boswick on a first date.

Except, there ain't gonna be a first date, he mused resolutely. *I'm through with dating and good-night kisses forever!*

"Thank you, Mr. Corbett," he heard Lydia say as her airy Southern voice wafted down from her porch.

He pivoted, facing her. "Alec, remember? My friends call me Alec."

"That's right." She smiled. "Thanks again, *Alec.*"

"Don't mention it. Only next time I'll remember my cape."

She momentarily frowned, obviously not understanding the joke. But suddenly she got it and burst into laughter so light-sounding and contagious it caused Alec to grin broadly.

"All right, *Superman,*" she quipped.

He chuckled and then couldn't resist asking the question on his mind ever since he saw the Lincoln pull into her driveway.

"Tell me something," he began, slowly striding toward her. "Why would a woman like you go out with a guy like. . .*Sim?*"

"A woman like me?" A puzzled frown marred her nicely shaped brows.

"Yeah. You seem like you're reasonably intelligent."

"Oh, thank you very much," she replied sarcastically.

Alec laughed at her reaction.

"If you must know, I went out with Simeon Crenshaw as a favor to my father-in-law. It was not of my own doing."

"Ah. I knew there had to be an explanation." He eyed her speculatively. "Can I ask you something else?"

Lydia nodded, albeit hesitantly.

"Speaking of your father-in-law, I read about him in tonight's newspaper. Is he really facing extortion charges?"

She sighed wearily. "I'm afraid so. This morning a reporter came to the office asking all sorts of questions and I really didn't get a chance to talk to Gerald about the whole situation until he came here tonight to pick up the children. That's when he told me about the district attorney's office threatening him with this awful business."

"Any truth to it?"

"Of course not. And my father-in-law has his attorneys working on the case already. In fact, Sim is one of his lawyers."

Alec mulled over the information, then smirked. "Well, he seems pushy enough to be a lawyer. Maybe he'll get your father-in-law off the hook."

"I have my doubts. And not all lawyers have to be 'pushy' to be successful. My late husband, Michael, for instance, was an attorney and he'd been thoughtful, caring, and respectful— nothing like Sim! In fact, I wish Gerald would consult with the firm my husband had worked for, but he refuses."

"Hmm. . ." Alec observed that it was the second time she'd brought up her deceased husband in conversation, causing him to question his husband-seeker theory about her again. "Well, Lydia—is it okay if I call you Lydia?"

"Yes," she said demurely.

"Well, Lydia," he began again, "I think I'll call it a night."

"Me, too."

After a parting smile, she reentered her house and Alec, feeling more curious than ever about his neighbor, made his way back home.

Tyler stood on the fence the next day after supper and watched Mr. Alec play basketball. "Now y'all let me do the talking, Brooke, you hear?"

She lifted her little nose as if to say she wouldn't listen.

"Brooke," he said in warning, "you'd better. . .else I'll tell Mama you threw away your green beans tonight when she wasn't looking."

"Okay," she replied with a pout.

"Hey, Mr. Alec," Tyler called across the yard, "can I ask you something?"

"Sure." Picking up his basketball and holding it against his hip with one arm, he walked to the fence. "What's up, kid?"

"Well," he hedged, "I just wondered. . .well, my grampa Boswick is a preacher, you know. . . ."

"Yeah, what about him?"

"Well, he says folks are gonna go either to heaven or hell after they die and, see, me and Brooke know we're goin' to heaven cuz we asked Jesus to save us. I was six and a half and she was—"

"Last summer," Brooke interrupted proudly. "I was just four and a half."

Tyler elbowed her to keep quiet. This was important! Mama wouldn't marry a man who wasn't a Christian, so Mr. Alec had to get saved.

"Anyway, me and Brooke want you to go to heaven after you die. Want to? I can tell you how to get born again. It's easy." Tyler nodded persuasively.

"Just ask Jesus into your heart to live forever," Brooke said. "But then you gotta read your Bible and pray every day so you grow, grow, grow."

Tyler gave his sister a scowl for reciting the words to that dumb song she learned in the kindergarten choir at church, but Mr. Alec started to laugh. Puzzled, he looked back at their neighbor.

"You kids are too much," he said, smiling. "But I appreciate the fact that you're concerned about my soul. That's good. Real good. Lots of people need the Lord, but I'm a Christian already. I got saved about five years ago."

Tyler widened his wondering gaze. "You did?"

Mr. Alec nodded.

"Awesome!"

"But I didn't see you at church on Sunday," Brooke told him.

"That's because I attend a different church."

Tyler frowned. A different church? That could mean trouble. Grampa wouldn't like it. He says other churches are "steeped in rebellion and pride." And Mama wouldn't leave SPCC. So Mr. Alec would have to make the switch. And maybe he would. . .once he and Mama got married. Oh, well, better leave that problem to the grown-ups, Tyler decided.

Tipping his head, Tyler studied the man before him. He wore blue jeans and a green sweatshirt with yellow letters across the front that read GREEN BAY PACKERS.

Mr. Alec caught him looking at it and grinned. "You like football, Ty?"

"Sure do."

"Yeah, me too."

"I don't like football," Brooke announced, shaking her blond head.

"That's cuz you're just a dumb girl."

She gasped. "I'm tellin' Mama!" She jumped off the fence and ran for the back door before Tyler could stop her.

"I hate sisters," he groused.

"Aw, now, Jesus wouldn't want you to hate her." Mr. Alec tousled his hair and chuckled. "But I know how you feel. I grew up with two *older* sisters. See, things could be worse."

"Tyler," Mama called from the back door. "Time to come in."

He sighed, knowing he was doomed. But he saw Mr. Alec wave in his mother's direction—and Tyler noticed that he kind of smiled, too. *He likes her!* Tyler thought, brightening.

"Tyler. . .right now, son."

"Yes, ma'am," he called back. He gazed up at his tall,

strong-looking new friend. "See y'all later. . .I hope."

As Tyler walked slowly toward his awaiting mother, he heard Mr. Alec call, "Go easy on the kid, Lydia. He's one man in a house full of women. Outnumbered. That'd be tough on any guy."

Mama gave him one of her looks—the one that meant she thought something was funny except she wasn't going to laugh. But she smiled in a way that made her cheeks pink.

She likes him, too. She does! She really does!

The back door closed and Tyler swung around to face his mother. "Upstairs to your room, young man," she commanded sternly. "And you may not use the computer tonight."

"But aren't you gonna go easy on me like Mr. Alec said?"

Mama's eyes narrowed slightly, and Tyler knew the answer before she even voiced it. "No."

Shoulders slumped, he turned and marched upstairs. *If Mr. Alec were my daddy,* he mused grumpily, *I'd be able to use my computer tonight.* In his room, he lay down on top of his bed, hands behind his head as he stared at the ceiling. *I gotta think of something. . . .*

He thought and thought, then suddenly he remembered a movie he'd seen at Matt's house once. It was about twin girls who were trying to get their mother and father back together again. He grinned, recalling some of their antics, and decided it wouldn't hurt to create a few of his own. Maybe if the sink got clogged again. . .or maybe. . .maybe. . .

He smiled broadly. *Yeah, that's it!*

six

Things were going from bad to worse—at least in Lydia's
estimation. Standing by the counter in her kitchen, she continued grating the cheddar cheese for tonight's supper and
rehashing the day's events in her mind.

Gerald had been charged with three counts of extortion. He'd
been fingerprinted and photographed like a common criminal,
and if all that weren't bad enough, the media seemed delighted
to broadcast the scandal. Reporters from both the local newspaper and television stations descended on the church that
afternoon. It had gotten so hectic, the Christian day school let
out early so the children wouldn't be exposed to any of the
malicious reports. Lydia had to admit that Sim Crenshaw han-
dled the press with tact and dignity, promising "his client"
would fight the slanderous lawsuit. But Lydia wondered if the
damage to Gerald's ministry hadn't already been done.

She glanced over her shoulder at the telephone, wondering
if she should call her mother. Her own mother. . .one of
Gerald's accusers. Unthinkable. But hadn't it been Mama's
new husband's fault? Pete Jackson? He was the kind of man
Gerald summed up from 2 Timothy 3: "For of this sort are
they which creep into houses, and lead captive silly women
laden with sins, led away with divers lusts, ever learning, and
never able to come to the knowledge of the truth." It had been
difficult for Lydia to accept, but she guessed Gerald was right.
Her mother was one of those "silly women."

Nevertheless, Lydia missed her terribly.

"Mama?" Brooke's sweet, childish voice broke into her troubled thoughts. "Can Tyler and me have candles for supper?"

"Candles?" Lydia grinned. "You mean candlelight while
you eat?"

Brooke nodded her blond head, wearing a wide smile.

It was a game they played sometimes, eating at the "restaurant" with candlelight, and Lydia hoped it taught her children good manners for when they'd experience the real thing.

"Sure, you can have candles for dinner," Lydia said. "In fact that might be the very thing to cheer me up, too."

Brooke ran outside and, watching through the kitchen window, Lydia saw her tell Tyler the news. He smiled triumphantly, whispered back to his little sister, and suddenly Lydia suspected those two were up to something. She glanced into Alec's backyard and didn't see him. *Good. At least they're not pestering him.* She shrugged it off, thinking her children were planning some kind of cute, little "surprise" as they often did.

Turning her attention back to making supper, Lydia sprinkled the grated cheese over the partially boiled macaroni, added butter, milk, mixed the ingredients well, and topped it off with bread crumbs. Finally, she slid the casserole into the oven.

Then she proceeded to set the table for two. Lydia just wasn't hungry tonight—she'd barely eaten all day, with all the commotion in her life. But she wanted to make the evening meal atmosphere pleasant and family-oriented tonight. They needed some semblance of normalcy in their lives. So she'd at least sit with Tyler and Brooke while they dined.

With her immediate tasks completed, at least for the next half hour while the casserole baked, Lydia returned her thoughts to whether she should phone her mother. More than ever, she felt stuck in the ugly crossfire between church and family.

"God wants us to be happy, Lydia," her mother had said when they'd last spoken—just before she'd been excommunicated. "Pete makes me happy. He's fun to be around, and he loves the Lord Jesus just as much as Gerald does. Why shouldn't I marry him? God's body of believers is not restricted to Southern Pride Community Church. I've realized what an ostrich I've been all these years. There are so many other Christians out there just as zealous and fervent as anyone at SPCC. Just remember that, Lydia. Remember that. . . ."

She shook herself from her musings in time to see Alec in her driveway with his toolbox in hand, heading for her back door. She frowned, wondering at his visit.

"Lydia?" he called through the screen before knocking loudly.

She walked to the door. "Hi. What's up?"

"I'm here to fix your sink." He opened the door and entered.

She frowned in confusion. "My sink?"

"Yeah. Didn't you send Tyler over to tell me that drain's giving you problems again?"

"No, I. . ." She watched him glance over at the table where two tapers stood in silver holders, awaiting a light. A Victorian rose-printed cloth covered the round table and places were set for two. Lydia felt herself blanch with embarrassment as the realization set in. "I think my son has outdone himself this time."

Alec looked back at her, a baffled expression on his face.

"I hate to tell you this, but, um, we've been set up. By an eight-year-old, who had some help from his little sister," Lydia said.

Alec set down his tools. "Oh, yeah?" By the glower on his face, Lydia could tell he didn't believe her. Most likely her neighbor thought *she* had arranged this little tête-à-tête.

"Look, I'm so sorry about this. My sink is not stopped up, and I'll see to it that Tyler is properly disciplined for his shenanigans. Brooke, too, for her part in it. Please, take your wrenches and pliers back home. I just feel terrible for bothering you, and on a Friday evening, too. I'm sure you've got plans." She stooped to lift the metal tool chest and hand it to him, but Alec quickly scooped it up.

"You know, Lydia," he said, wagging a long finger at her, "that kid of yours. . ."

He suddenly burst into chuckles and Lydia nearly fainted with relief. *He's not angry. Thank You, Lord.*

"Lydia," he began again, "that kid's precocious now, but just wait till he's a teenager. Then what are you going to do?"

She shrugged helplessly. "Lock him in his room till he's twenty-one? I don't know."

"Good luck."

Lydia managed a weak smile. "I'm sorry, Alec."

"No harm done, I guess." He raised a brow as if in after-thought. "But it was Tyler who concocted this and not you, right? I mean, this isn't some kind of plot to lure me into your house for an impromptu romantic dinner, using your kids' little prank as the bait. . .is it?"

Stunned by the accusation, Lydia was rendered momentarily speechless. "I'd never devise a plan to entice a man into my home. If I wanted a dinner guest, I'd just send an invitation."

Alec nodded, while eyeing her speculatively. "And this wasn't your way of 'sending' out the invite, huh?"

"No, this wasn't it." Indignation quickly set in. "And for your information, I have more integrity than to use my children for anything sneaky and underhanded. I'm only sorry you have such a dark opinion of my character."

"Look, Lydia, I didn't mean to insult you, but I wasn't sure. I've been the recipient of this kind of thing far too often. I dislike being set up and I hate blind dates."

"Ditto." She placed her hand on his upper arm and gave him a push toward the door, though it didn't even budge him. "Good night," she said tersely, "and, again, I apologize for the inconvenience."

He turned and left peaceably without another word, and after soundly closing the door behind him, Lydia sagged against it. She squeezed her eyes together, forestalling the urge to break down and sob. How could Alec have insinuated she was some kind of Jezebel? She felt humiliated to the depth of her being.

"Mama?"

Glancing across the room, she saw Tyler and Brooke standing in the hallway near the kitchen entrance. Their small faces had worry lines creasing their brows.

"That was not nice, you two."

The children had the good grace to look contrite.

"Go wash up and I'll serve supper," she instructed. "And while you eat, you're both going to have a lesson on proper manners concerning next-door neighbors."

"Yes, ma'am," they replied as one before heading to the bathroom.

"And, Tyler?"

He paused. "Yes?"

"You are not to speak to that man again, do you understand? Furthermore, tomorrow morning you're going to give that bicycle back."

"But, Mama—"

"Don't you argue with me. My mind's made up."

The boy's face fell. "Yes, ma'am."

ða

As Alec put dishes away in the kitchen cupboards, he spied Lydia through his window above the sink. It faced directly into her kitchen and, although there was a good deal of distance between them, Alec had a clear view as long as she didn't close her blinds.

Curious, he stood there watching. She sat across the table from her kids whose backs were to him, and she appeared to be in serious discussion. As far as he could tell, she wasn't raising her voice as some mothers were known to do, but at the same time, Alec instinctively knew Tyler and Brooke were getting a thorough reprimand.

He'd like to laugh off the whole incident, but his conscience sorely pricked him. He shouldn't have confronted Lydia the way he did. She had looked as though she were going to cry. And he might have been tempted to think tears were part of the ploy, except something in her dusky eyes said otherwise.

Women. Go figure. His thoughts floated back.

When he'd met Denise shortly after becoming a Christian, he knew immediately she was the one for him. Denise with her stunning long, blond hair and big baby blues. He would have lassoed the moon for her—he'd been that captivated by the woman—and he had thought she felt the same. So when she broke their engagement, saying she'd "changed her mind," Alec thought she was kidding. But she wasn't, and within a week of their breakup, Denise had found someone new from their singles group at church. Unable to bear watching the romance unfold before his eyes, Alec decided to leave—first the church, then Milwaukee, and finally the whole state of Wisconsin. He'd left family behind, but they had never been closely knit. His parents divorced when Alec and his sisters were young; they'd been shuffled from mother to father and back to their mother again. No, there hadn't been anything or anybody standing in Alec's way once he'd made up his mind to leave.

But now that he was here, he didn't quite know how to deal with his pretty new neighbor. Oh, he felt attracted to her, no doubt about it, except he sure wished he didn't. Besides, he'd learned beauty was only skin deep and he wasn't about to make another mistake and fall headlong in love with some fickle-minded woman, like Denise, who'd break his heart again.

It's best Lydia thinks I'm a jerk, he decided, turning away from the window and resuming his task of unpacking his kitchen. *Then she'll hate me, and she'll stay away. Good. That's just fine by me.*

❧

The next morning Alec awoke to the sun streaming through his bedroom window. Another glorious day in the South. He dressed and straightened up a bit, reminding himself the Singles Group from church was meeting at his house tonight for a Bible study. Around noon, he ambled outside into his backyard, deciding to cut the lawn. He'd just pulled the mower out of the garage, when he spotted Lydia and Tyler walking up his driveway wheeling along the new bike he'd given the kid last week.

"Good morning," he called, still feeling a bit sheepish for his bad behavior yesterday.

Lydia smiled a taut greeting as he strode across the grass to meet them.

"Hi, Tyler."

"Hi." The boy glanced down at his tennis shoes.

"We came to give the bicycle back to you," his mother began. She wore a short-sleeved denim dress with little pink flowers sewn onto its bodice and Alec noticed its color made her eyes look bluer. . .or was that anger darkening her gaze? "Tyler really has all the toys he needs," she drawled, "and he has a bicycle. We decided this should go to somebody who doesn't own one already."

"Hmm. . ." Alec looked at the boy, still studying the pavement.

"But we appreciate your generosity all the same. . .don't we, Ty?"

"Yeah," he replied, sounding less than enthused.

"Look, Lydia, if this is about last night—"

"Take the bike," she said curtly, pushing it toward him. "We don't want it." She put an arm around her son's drooping shoulders. "Come along, Ty."

As they retreated down the driveway, Alec stood there holding onto the handlebars, watching them go. Lydia had put her thick chestnut mane in some sort of clip at the back of her head, and her hair bobbed with each irritated step she took. "Aren't you making a little too much of this?" he couldn't help but call after her.

She stopped short. Turning to Tyler, she sent him on his way before spinning on her heel and marching back toward him.

Alec wanted to chuckle, except he knew from the determined expression on her face that he was about to get a good tongue-lashing. However, when she reached him, she seemed to swallow whatever she really wanted to say and, instead, smiled up at him kindly.

"I know you can't help it, Mr. Corbett."

He arched a brow. "Help what?"

"Your rude behavior. Your bitter attitude. Since I am surrounded by Christians at work all week long, and seeing as my friends are believers, I forget what the world is really like. But the Lord Jesus Christ can make a difference in your life. He made a difference in mine."

Alec smirked. "I'm a believer. You're preaching to the choir, honey."

"Yes, well," she glanced down momentarily before meeting his gaze once more. "Tyler told me you said you were a Christian, but just going to a church doesn't make you a born-again child of God. It's not about a religion, it's about a relationship with the Savior."

"Lydia, I am a born again believer. I got saved five years ago."

Confusion crossed her pretty face. "But you don't act like it, and Jesus said we would know fellow believers by their fruit."

"Listen, don't you dare stand in judgment of me," he stated harshly. "You don't even know me."

"But you stand in judgment of me and you don't know me, either."

Alec brought his chin up sharply as her comment met its mark.

"Now, as you're aware, we're having a little trouble at our church," she said in that sweet southern voice of hers. "Some resentful former members are out to get my father-in-law, but he is a good preacher and I'd like to invite you to come out and hear him tomorrow morning."

"I attend another church, but thanks," Alec replied dryly.

Lydia just nodded before walking away. Again, Alec watched her go, but this time he didn't feel as remorseful about having offended her as he did about having offended the Lord, Himself.

seven

"Boy, Alec, some neighbor you are. I'm glad you don't live next door to me!"

He looked over at the woman with short, light brown hair, sitting sideways in a chair, her jean-encased legs dangling over its arm. "Thanks, Debbie," he replied sarcastically. "I knew I could count on you for some encouragement."

The young woman laughed as did several of his other friends. Since they began tonight's Bible study with prayer requests, Alec mentioned Lydia, the situation with her father-in-law, and then before he knew it, he'd spilled the whole story—how he'd fixed her sink, come to her rescue last Monday night, and finally how he had insulted her character and she, in return, had doubted his faith.

He sighed heavily. "I feel doubly bad," he added, "because Lydia has told her kids they can't speak to me. Poor Tyler. . . you should have seen him out in his yard this afternoon. He seemed miserable. He's just dying for some male companionship, not to mention the fact that he's mourning the loss of a new bike."

"Well, there's a reason why God moved you in next door," dark-headed Larry said, lifting another slice of pizza out of the box sitting on the coffee table. "Maybe He wants you to be a father figure to the boy."

"Too late now," Alec replied. "I blew it."

"Did you try apologizing?" Debbie asked sarcastically.

Alec clenched his jaw, but he had to confess—he hadn't.

"Why don't you go over right now and tell your neighbor you're sorry?" Judy suggested, folding her leg beneath her as she sat on the floor near Debbie. She flipped a portion of her long hair over her shoulder.

"Yeah. . .wouldn't want the sun to go down on your anger," Tim said from his place on the sofa next to Alec. "Or hers."

Alec shook his head. "If I go over there, Lydia will most likely slam the door in my face. And I'd deserve it."

"Regardless of her reaction," Debbie stated bluntly, "you still have an obligation to do what's right."

"Hey, who invited you tonight, anyway?" Alec teased, grinning all the while.

"Go on, Alec," Judy prodded. "And after you make amends, invite her to our Bible study."

"She won't come. Her kids are probably asleep and Lydia told me she doesn't like to leave them unattended, even to walk next door."

"Well, if she's Gerald Boswick's daughter-in-law," Larry put in, "she most likely won't come just because we're not a part of Southern Pride Community Church. They think they're the only ones going to heaven."

"Hmm. . ." Alec mulled over the remark, wondering if that was the real reason Lydia had doubted his faith.

"Hold on, you guys," Debbie said, "we're getting off track. The problem isn't Lydia, it's Alec. He did wrong and he's got to apologize." She gave him a pointed stare. "So, go on. Git."

"You know," Alec said, rising from the sofa, "I think you need to practice some of that meek and quiet spirit stuff."

"Which is in the sight of God of great price," Tim added, pushing his wire-rim glasses higher up on his nose. He was always the one to quote Scripture.

Debbie threw her empty Styrofoam cup at the both of them and everyone laughed again.

≈

Lydia sat on the couch with the cordless phone in her lap. Beside her was her address book, containing her mother's new phone number. Should she call? What would she say?

Lord, I feel like a little girl who's missing her mama. She picked up the receiver, but then set it down again. She couldn't decide.

The front doorbell rang, causing Lydia to jump. Slowly, she rose from the immaculate, cream upholstered sofa and padded in her stocking feet to the living room window. She peeked out through the lacy sheers. *Alec. What does he want?*

Reluctantly, she went to the door and pulled hard on the knob, simultaneously donning her best hostess expression. "Well, Mr. Corbett," she greeted. "What a surprise."

"Can the 'Mr. Corbett' stuff, Lydia. I came here to apologize."

She took a deep breath, bracing herself. This man, while handsome enough, possessed an abrasive demeanor and his presence threatened her fragile composure at the moment. She could scarcely believe she'd had the courage to stand up to him this morning.

"I shouldn't have said what I did last night," he began, his voice sounding softer. Lydia noticed his eyes. She had thought they were plain brown, a lighter shade than her children's dark gazes, but she'd been mistaken. They were the color of topaz, and beneath her porch light they shone with sincerity. "I guess I'm one of those guys once bitten, twice shy, as the old cliché goes. And you were right. I've been standing in judgment of you, using the same measuring stick I hold to the woman who hurt me. That wasn't fair. I'm sorry."

Unsure of her emotions, Lydia merely nodded. On one hand, she felt taken aback by his humility, on the other, she was grateful for his candidness.

"How 'bout we call a truce, okay?" Alec stuck out his right hand.

She smiled. How could she help it? When he put his mind to it, this man could be downright charming. "All right. Truce." She slipped her hand into his much larger one.

Alec gave it a gentle squeeze and grinned. "Truce." Then, much to her surprise, he didn't let it go. "Say, listen, some friends from church and I are having a Bible study. Want to join us?"

"I can't," she replied, feeling oddly disappointed. "Tyler and Brooke are sleeping."

At last, he released her hand. "Yeah, I figured, but I thought I'd invite you anyhow."

Lydia managed a weak smile as Alec sharpened his gaze and searched her face.

"You weren't. . .crying, were you?"

"No. I think I'm catching a cold," she fibbed. In truth, she'd been sobbing on and off all day—whenever she thought the kids wouldn't see. But she hadn't expected her new neighbor to be so perceptive and now she felt embarrassed. Were her eyes still red? Her face puffy? Good night! Why had she even answered the door?

"Yeah, well, I heard there's a flu bug going around."

Lydia nodded. "And you'd better put on a coat," she advised in her strongest voice, "or you're liable to catch pneumonia."

"Are you kidding?" Alec chuckled, and she thought it had a nice, happy sound to it. He didn't appear quite so formidable when he smiled, either. "It's fifty-five degrees out here. That's practically summer to me."

She folded her arms, feeling chilled to the bone. "Then you'll positively melt when it's July and one hundred degrees in the shade."

"You're probably right. But I'd rather melt than freeze to death." He smiled at her again. "Well, I'd better get back. See ya, Lydia."

She smiled back. "See ya."

She watched him walk away—Alec in his purple-and-green long-sleeved shirt with THE MILWAUKEE BUCKS printed across the front. *At least it's neatly tucked into his blue jeans*, she thought, closing the door. He might be a casual dresser, but he never looked like a slob. Walking farther into the living room, she allowed her gaze to fall on the telephone. *You'd like him, Mama. You'd like Alec Corbett. In a way, he reminds me of Michael.*

eight

Alec reentered his house and all eyes turned on him.

"So?" Debbie asked. "What happened?"

"I apologized and everything's fine." His friends cheered and Alec couldn't help a grin, although inside he felt sorry for Lydia. She'd been crying, all right. He could tell. He'd grown up with sisters and he knew the signs. What's more, she looked like she might have enjoyed some company tonight.

"Did you invite her to the Bible study?" Judy asked.

"Yeah, but just like I told you, her kids are sleeping."

"And it's probably too late to get a baby-sitter," Debbie remarked. She lifted a contemplative brow. "But we could take our Bible study over to her place. You think she'd be interested, Alec?"

"Yeah, I think Lydia might be interested."

"No kidding?" Larry feigned a shocked expression. "A Boswick wants to attend a Bible study outside of SPCC? I'm about to have heart failure!"

Alec shot him a quelling look. "She didn't exactly say she wanted to attend. It's just a hunch."

"Judy, let's you and me go over and ask," Debbie suggested, getting up from the armchair.

"Maybe I'd better go along," Alec said.

"Why don't we all just go over, and if she says no, we'll come back here," Tim proposed.

"You don't think we'll scare her, do you?" Judy asked seriously. "I mean, if a group of strangers knocked on my door and asked to come in for a Bible study, I'd feel a little nervous."

"Well, Alec will be there," Debbie reasoned, picking up her Bible. "She knows him, right?"

"Sort of," he said. "We've only been neighbors for a week."

"Good enough. Larry, you take the pizza. Tim, you bring the pop. Everyone got their Bibles? Okay. Come on, gang," Debbie ordered, "let's go."

Out she marched, leading the way, and Alec shook his head as he followed. *Bossy woman. . .*

❧

Lydia ditched her ideas about phoning her mother and started turning off lights beginning in the den. Glancing around the room and making sure everything was in its place, Lydia switched off the lamp. The darkness of the room increased her loneliness and for a brief moment, she thought it might consume her. She felt disconnected from the total universe. Friends had become scarce over the years since many people seemed intimidated by the fact that she was a Boswick. She spent most of her life at church, surrounded by its members. And the women there were cordial, but distant. Men, in general, were polite and those who were single voiced their desire to date her, although none of them piqued Lydia's interest. The only man who caused her head to turn lately was her new neighbor. But she scarcely knew him, other than that he came from up north and had an intense aversion to blind dates. What had he said? He'd been hurt?

Mulling over his apology, Lydia walked into the living room as the doorbell rang again, but this time when she peeked out the curtains, she saw more than just Alec standing on her porch. Intuitively, she knew he was accompanied by the "friends" he'd mentioned when he invited her to the Bible study. But what did they want with her? More than curious, she walked to the door and opened it.

"Hi," said a short-haired woman wearing jeans and a T-shirt. "I'm Debbie Thompson and this is Judy Landers, Larry Matthews, Tim Parker. . .and you know Alec."

Lydia managed a polite smile, nodding at everyone. "Hi," she replied.

"Alec had an inkling you might like to join our Bible study tonight, and since you don't have a baby-sitter, we figured we'd come on over to your place. That is, if you really want to participate. We'd love it if you would, but we don't want to intrude if you're busy."

"Well, I. . ." Surprised by the offer, Lydia didn't know what to say. She glanced at Alec, who stood off to the side.

He smiled easily. "Just thought maybe you'd appreciate some Christian fellowship tonight."

"We're not part of a cult or anything, looking for converts," Tim told her, "so don't get scared. All of us are from Berean Baptist Church. Ever heard of it?"

"Yes, as a matter of fact, I know your pastor." Lydia recalled an evening long ago when Mark Spencer and his wife, Jerrica Dawn, attended a dinner party right here at her house. Lydia remembered the pastor as a man with an easy smile and a solid faith.

"Well, what's it gonna be? Pizza's getting cold," Larry said, prompting her decision.

Lydia laughed softly in spite of herself. "Sure. Come on in. Alec's right," she said, casting a glance his way. "I'm in the mood for some company."

The group of five filed into the foyer, oohing and aahing over her awesome house.

"Please, come in and make yourselves comfortable," Lydia invited, showing them into the living room.

"It looks so perfect in here that I'm afraid to sit down on the furniture," said Judy. She was a plump woman, but nice looking, and Lydia found herself impressed by her hair. It hung in dark blond waves that fell past her hips.

"Nonsense," she replied. "My children are known for jumping all over it."

She heard Alec's deep chuckle as he walked into the room, and she felt immensely relieved that the animosity between them had dissipated. Watching him settle into the couch, she tried to imagine why and how he'd been hurt before. Once bitten, twice shy—wasn't that what he'd said? Lydia suddenly found herself longing to prove the old "love of a good woman" theory true—except she couldn't understand her feelings. They barely knew each other. Still, there was just something about him. . .

"Oh, wow," Debbie exclaimed, drawing Lydia's attention away from Alec, "look at this fireplace." She whirled around. "Let's make a fire. I live in an apartment. I never get to enjoy such a luxury. But don't worry," she stated hastily, "I'll start it. You just sit down and relax, Lydia. I'll take care of everything."

"I'd better do it," Alec remarked, standing. "I don't want you burning this whole house down."

"Oh, quiet. I know what I'm doing," Debbie insisted.

"Lydia," Alec asked, turning toward her, "is it all right with you?"

Lydia nodded, relishing the thought of a cozy fire as they studied God's Word.

He leaned forward. "Listen, don't mind Debbie," he whispered. "She could make a Marine cower."

"I heard that, Alec," the short-haired woman stated over her shoulder while hunkering in front of the stone hearth.

Everyone chuckled at the exchange, including Lydia. "Well," she managed at last, "I'll go get some plates for the pizza and glasses and ice for the pop." Turning, she headed for the kitchen.

"Allow me to help you," Larry called from behind her.

"Well, thank you," she replied gratefully.

In the kitchen, she pulled out a large serving tray before collecting the necessary items and handing them to Larry, who carried everything back into the living room.

"Maybe we should all introduce ourselves for Lydia's sake," Judy suggested from her place in one of the swivel rockers. Larry took the other matching rocker, and Debbie sat on the floor by the fire, which was well on its way. Tim and Alec were seated at opposite ends of the couch, leaving the middle cushion vacant, so Lydia politely settled herself in between the two men.

"Ladies first," Tim said, "and since you came up with the

idea, why don't you begin, Judy?"

"Okeydokey."

Judy gave a brief autobiography, including salvation testimony.

"Lydia, you're our hostess, so you go next."

She looked across the room at Debbie and shrugged. "Not much to tell. I've lived in North Carolina all my life. I became a Christian at nine years old and met my husband when I was sixteen. We dated until I was twenty-one, and then we had eight blissful years of marriage before God took Michael home. I'm a widow now, but I'm thankful that I've got two precious children, ages eight and five."

"Do you work outside the home?" Larry asked.

"Yes. I'm a secretary at Southern Pride Community Church."

"And your father-in-law is *the* Gerald Boswick," Tim added. "Didn't he write a book awhile ago? He's pretty well known, especially around here."

"Yes, he's authored several books," Lydia stated, turning toward the man with the strawberry blond hair and glasses, sitting to her right.

"Hey, is all that true about him? His fall from grace, so to speak? Boy, there's an example of how power and money'll lead a man down the path of destruction." Larry sat forward in his chair, reaching for a slice of pizza. He was a fairly nice-looking man, in Lydia's opinion, with his slim build, dark brown hair, and hazel eyes. But his comment caused her to bristle.

"The allegations against my father-in-law are vicious lies!" she declared, hearing the terseness in her own voice. The room grew uncomfortably quiet and Larry had the good grace to look chagrined. Then Alec stretched his arm across the back of couch just behind her in a reassuring gesture. Lydia suddenly felt foolish for her display of emotion. "I'm sorry," she said, examining her folded hands. "It's just very upsetting."

"Nothing for you to be sorry about," Alec stated. "Larry was out of line."

"I was," he admitted. "Forgive me. Guess I wasn't thinking."

Lydia managed a tight smile, willing herself not to burst into tears.

Alec's arm came down around her, his hand briefly touching her shoulder consolingly before he stood. "Want some pop? Hey, Debbie, pour some pop into that glass and hand it to me."

"Yes, sir, Mr. Drill Sergeant," she quipped, although she readily complied.

Laughingly, Judy turned to Lydia. "Since the day these two met, they've been on each other's case."

"Yeah, the last two Saturday nights, they've sort of been our entertainment," Tim added, wearing a wide grin.

"I pity you, living next door to him," Debbie told Lydia. "I'll pray for you daily."

Lydia couldn't help feeling amused as Alec handed her the glass. "Hey, don't smile at her wisecracks," he said with an indignant expression. Just when Lydia was about to apologize, he sent her a wink.

She sipped her soda while Alec sat back down beside her.

Debbie introduced herself next. She was born and raised in New York City and got transferred to Charlotte eighteen months ago. "It's been quite an adjustment for me," she confessed. "But I'm really beginning to like it down here."

Then came Larry's turn, followed by Tim's, and as Lydia heard their testimonies, she felt impressed by them. They really were committed Christians. Other than their pastor, she hadn't met people with such a strong faith outside of her own church in a long while. She wondered why Gerald was so adamant about not fellowshipping with those from other churches, and she also found herself recalling Michelle Marx's questions. *Is it true that many more women are accepted into the fold here at Southern Pride Community Church than are men? Is it true that scores of men are turned away from this church every year because Pastor Boswick will not abide anyone disagreeing with his theology? Is it true? Is it true?*

Of course not, Lydia thought, shifting slightly on the couch, and yet she tumultuously wondered if the three men sitting in her living room tonight would be "accepted into the fold." She had a feeling they would not. They didn't seem the SPCC type. Then, again, neither had Michael, and that "perfect man syndrome," as he called it, had always irked him. He often said some of the men at SPCC were nothing more than "plastic people." Until now, however, Lydia hadn't paid much attention to his remarks, thinking he'd made them in jest. *And hadn't he?*

"I'm from Milwaukee, Wisconsin," Alec began, pulling Lydia from her reverie. "I was engaged to be married, but it busted up and I felt like starting over someplace new. So I put in for a transfer at work and wound up here. My first week in Woodruff has been. . .interesting. Guess I didn't make a great first impression on my neighbor." He gave Lydia a hooded glance and she felt herself blush. "But my job's going well. I think I'll stick around awhile."

"What's your occupation?" Lydia asked curiously.

"I'm a carpenter and I'm employed by a national firm that does a lot of cabinetry work—especially in new homes."

"A carpenter? Really?" Lydia smiled. "We sure could have used your help around here when we first bought this place."

He chuckled. "Yeah, I imagine."

"A carpenter," she repeated somewhat reverently. "After fixing up this house, I certainly have a great respect for men who work with wood. Besides, it's quite likely that Jesus was a carpenter before He began His ministry."

"Oh, why'd you have to say that?" Debbie groaned. "I can see Alec's ego inflating before my very eyes."

"You're just jealous," he shot back, wearing a wry grin.

"Of you? Hardly."

"Children, children," Larry said exaggeratedly with uplifted hands. "We're here to have a Bible study, remember? What will Miss Lydia think?"

"A good thing she's used to kids," Tim muttered glibly.

And on and on it went. Soon Lydia found herself giggling until her eyes teared. She couldn't remember the last time she'd had such a good laugh.

Finally, they got down to the whole purpose of the evening. Alec offered to share his Bible with Lydia so she wouldn't have to get up and fetch hers. Tim led the study of Isaiah 40:28–31. Tying it in with the theme of singleness, he concluded, "If we trust the Lord to bring the right person into our lives, He'll give us His strength and we won't 'faint' while we wait—in other words, we won't be discouraged while we wait on Him."

"What if He never does bring someone into your life?" Lydia asked sincerely.

"Weeks ago, we did a study of Psalm 37," Judy explained, "and determined that if God has placed a desire in our hearts to marry, He will make it happen. We just need to trust Him for the right timing—and the right one."

"And in the case of my broken engagement," Alec added candidly, "I realized tonight I need to trust that God made the right decision there. I know He never makes mistakes, but it's taken me all these months to accept the fact that He *allowed* it to happen. . .for my own good."

"That's right," Larry said.

"And what about your husband's death, Lydia?" Debbie asked. "Have you been able to accept it?"

"Oh yes. I accepted it long ago. I know Michael is in a place so wonderful he wouldn't come back here to me and the children for anything. Besides, the Bible says a day with the Lord is like a thousand on earth. Michael will meet the Savior and then look over his shoulder and there we'll be."

"But what about you?" Judy asked, looking concerned.

"Me? Oh, I'm all right." Despite her guests' ability to wear their hearts on their sleeves, Lydia couldn't get herself to admit to the loneliness that frequently haunted her.

"I'm sure you get plenty of support from your church, huh?" Larry asked.

"Yes, that's right," Lydia replied. "I'm most grateful to my father-in-law for all his care of Tyler, Brooke, and me."

There was a moment's pause and then Tim began speaking about a young woman with whom he worked. He was interested in her, but she didn't know the Lord. . .yet. Next Debbie talked about a man she'd met through the Internet. Was it safe for singles to meet each other on the web? Was it of God?

It was nearly midnight when they wrapped up their topics and closed in prayer. Lydia felt as though she'd gotten more out of this casual Bible study and its following discussion than she did a month's worth of Sunday morning sermons.

"I'm glad y'all came over tonight," she drawled, seeing them to the door.

"Well, how 'bout next Saturday night, too?" Debbie asked. "Can you get a sitter?"

"Perhaps. I'll do my best."

"It's at my apartment," Debbie said. "Alec will give you my address and phone number if you want to come."

"Bossy," Alec muttered. Looking at Lydia, he said, "But, yes, I will give you the information."

"Thank you."

Bidding her new friends farewell, Lydia closed the front door after they left. She proceeded to clear the dishes and empty boxes of pizza, thinking how much she'd enjoyed their company tonight. And Alec. . .she had certainly seen a different side of him. Beneath that gruff exterior beat a tender heart.

With everything cleaned up, she sat back down in the living room and watched the last of the embers in the fireplace die out. Maybe she wouldn't mind remarrying after all—if the Lord brought about the right one. But Alec Corbett? He couldn't possibly be a running candidate for her husband. Gerald would never approve of him. He wasn't a member of SPCC, for one thing. Besides, what on earth was she thinking? She barely knew the man!

"Mama?"

Lydia snapped from her musings. "Tyler. What are you doing awake at this hour?"

"I've been awake a long time," he said, coming down the stairs slowly. "Who were all those people?"

"Just some friends. We had a Bible study tonight."

"Oh." Tyler paused, looking confused. "Mama, I saw you sitting next to Mr. Alec and smiling. You're not mad at him anymore, huh?"

"No. I'm not mad at him anymore."

He immediately beamed. "Cool!"

"Shh. . .you're going to wake up Brooke."

The boy broke into a whisper. "Sorry, Mama, but I've been praying and praying that you wouldn't be angry with Mr. Alec anymore."

"Seems God answered your prayers," she said, turning off the living room light. She slipped her arm around Tyler's shoulders as she walked him upstairs.

"Does that mean I can still talk to him?"

"Yes. But, Ty, you mustn't try to create situations to get Mr. Alec and me together."

"Like last night?"

"Yes. That was wrong of you and Brooke, just like we talked about at the supper table. If the Lord wants Mr. Alec. . . or anyone else to have a part of our lives, then we need to let Him work everything out."

Tyler searched her face as they stood at his bedroom door. "You like him, don't you, Mama?"

She tried not to grin at the direct question that caught her somewhat off guard. Still, she had a hard time hiding her feelings.

"You do! I knew it!"

"Shh. . .lower your voice."

He ran into his room, leaping into his bed. "I knew it!"

Lydia suddenly felt nervous—she didn't want her in-laws privy to this new, unexpected turn of her heart, and she certainly didn't want Alec to know. He'd most likely decide his initial suspicions of her were correct.

"Tyler," she said, padding across the carpeted floor and sitting on the edge of his bed, "let's just keep this a secret between you and me, all right?"

"Why?"

"Because God has to work in Mr. Alec's heart first. Right now all we can do is pray. . .and not say a word to *anyone*. Then, if something happens, we'll know for sure it's the Lord's will."

"Okay. I promise."

She smiled at his exuberance.

"God likes to answer my prayers."

"Yes, He sure does," Lydia admitted, standing and making her way out of the room.

"Grampa says God's gonna use me in a big way."

"I believe that." She blew him a kiss. "Good night. I love you."

"Love you, too."

Walking toward her own bedroom, Lydia couldn't suppress the chuckle bubbling up inside her. The future suddenly seemed to sparkle again. For the first time in two and a half years, she felt alive. Had she really been only existing for the sake of her children and others? No wonder Gerald had been concerned, telling her she should remarry. She'd been lifeless.

She strolled to the window and pulled back the blinds. *But everything changed in a week*, she thought incredulously, peering down at Alec's house. *All because a neighbor moved in next door*. Shaking her head, she added silently, *Alec Corbett, why do you make me feel like I'm a hopeful sixteen-year-old again?*

nine

Days passed and the rain began. The cold dampness had a way of creeping into the bones, not to mention the mind and spirit. For the first time in twelve years, Lydia felt sorry for her mother-in-law. The scandal surrounding Gerald leveled her to a mere shadow of the strong-willed, opinionated woman Lydia had known. She hadn't even fallen apart like this after losing her only son. But by the worship service on Thursday evening, Elberta had had more than she could bear and packed her bags and flew off to Tallahassee to stay indefinitely with her daughter, Mary. At church there were murmurs of Gerald's resignation—at least temporarily, until the talk quieted, Elberta returned, and the charges against him were dismissed. Gerald stubbornly refused to give in, saying he'd "raised this church up from the ground," but he acknowledged his need for some time away. On Friday morning, Sim obtained permission from the DA and Gerald left at noon for his secluded cabin in the Smoky Mountains. After he'd gone, Lydia wished there were something she could do for her in-laws. Things at SPCC seemed to be unraveling like a cheap sweater, and that afternoon as she drove home with Tyler and Brooke, she felt as bleak as the gloomy winter weather.

"Hey, Lydia," Alec called out his back door as she began to run for the house in the freezing downpour, "I want to talk to you. Can I come over? Won't take long."

"Sure," she said, reaching the back door and fishing in her purse for her keys.

"Hurry," Brooke whined, "I'm getting wet."

Lydia unlocked the door and the three of them spilled into the house. "What a day," she said with a long sigh.

Removing their wet things, the children agreed.

"Maybe we'll order a pizza for supper tonight."

"Yeah! And maybe Mr. Alec will stay and eat with us."

"Tyler, don't start. We talked about this, remember?"

He nodded grimly and followed his sister into the den. Still in the kitchen, Lydia heard the television go on. She rolled her head in a circle, stretching her tense neck muscles. This hadn't been a good day, and she wondered what Alec wanted. She hadn't seen him all week.

As if on cue, the doorbell rang and Tyler ran to answer it. "Hi, Mr. Alec," she heard him say. "Come on in."

"Hey, kid, how you doing?"

"Okay."

"Got your ark built yet?" Meeting him in the foyer, Lydia saw Alec chuckle while confusion flittered across Tyler's face. "Ark, get it?" he explained. "Like Noah and all the rain. . ."

"Oh!" The boy laughed.

Smiling, Alec looked over at Lydia. Clad in blue jeans and a striped, long-sleeve, button-down shirt, he made an impressive sight there in her hallway. Just seeing him again caused her a small measure of happiness after enduring the last seven hours at work.

"How are you?"

"Good," she fibbed. "And yourself?"

"Fine. I had a short day. Got off at noon." He scratched his jaw and shifted his stance uncomfortably.

Lydia glanced at Tyler, who watched the exchange with interest. Brooke, sitting on one of the sofas in the den, seemed to care less that their neighbor had stopped by and looked completely absorbed by the cartoon, sing-along video on TV.

"Alec, why don't you and I talk in the kitchen," she said, realizing he wanted to speak with her privately. "Tyler, you go back in the den."

"But, Mama—"

"Tyler." She gave him a direct look and he didn't argue.

"Yes, ma'am."

Alec grinned. "Kitchen's fine."

Turning, Lydia led the way. "I think I'll make some herbal tea. Would you like a cup?"

"Naw. Thanks anyway. This really won't take long. I just wondered if. . .um. . ." They reached the kitchen, and Lydia stopped by the counter, giving him her full attention. "Well, tomorrow is February thirteenth and the company I work for is throwing a Valentine's Day party. I normally wouldn't go, but being the new guy, I sort of feel obligated and I, um, need a date. If I show up without one, Norm Whitehall says he'll fix me up with his sister and if she resembles Norm even a little. . . Lydia this isn't funny. Quit laughing."

"I'm sorry," she said, doing her best to swallow her giggles. "It's been a long day and I guess I'm punchy." In truth, she felt a bit giddy that Alec was asking her out—even if it was in order to escape a blind date.

"Lydia, I wondered if maybe you'd go to the party with me," he asked, looking stone faced, but very vulnerable.

"I would be honored," she said.

He relaxed visibly. "Thanks."

"What time will you pick me up?"

"How's seven sound?"

"Fine." She smiled and then remembered their previous plans. "What about the Bible study?"

"Would you mind skipping it with me this week?"

Lydia shook her head.

"Sorry this is such short notice, but it took me four days to work up the courage to ask you."

"Oh, Alec. . ." She waved a hand at him. "I don't bite. Honest."

He laughed curtly. "Well, if you bit me, you'd have every good reason, considering the things I've said to you."

"I forgot all about them."

"Oh, yeah?" Pursing his lips, Alec scrutinized her in a way that caused Lydia's cheeks to warm.

She turned away. "Are you sure you don't want some tea?"

"Yeah. I'd better go." He walked back through the house to

the foyer, then stopped short. "On second thought. . ." He spun around.

Right behind him, Lydia halted midstride and arched questioning brows.

"I might be pushing my luck here, but would you and the kids want to go out for pizza tonight?"

Tyler whooped from the den. "Say yes, Mama!"

Lydia rolled her eyes at her son's response, but inside, her heart beat with as much enthusiasm. "Sure," she said at last, "we'd love to."

⁂

It was ten o'clock that night when Alec finally arrived back home. He tossed his truck keys onto his kitchen counter and stared at them as though they might come to life and turn somersaults. *I'm doing it again*, he thought almost miserably. *I'm falling head over heels in love with a woman—the very thing I vowed I wouldn't do.* He sighed, glancing at the ceiling. "Two weeks, Lord," he muttered in prayer. "Do you see what I've done in two short weeks? Got myself in another fine mess."

He sauntered through the house and into the living room, feeling a surge of disbelief shoot through him. Lydia Boswick—he didn't even know her middle name. He didn't know much about her at all, other than she owned and refurbished the house next door, was a widow, a Christian. . .and liked pizza. And she sure could talk, but that was all right with him. Tyler and Brook had been well-mannered at the table, and they obviously liked him—and, better yet, so did their mother.

Alec sat down on the couch and turned on the television set, mindlessly watching in muted silence whatever happened to be on. That Lydia shared his romantic interest, well, that made things easier. Wouldn't be hard to win her heart. But did he want to? In his experience, romances always started off all warm and fuzzy only to become complicated matters that messed with his mind and tore at his emotions. But there was always the chance this time could be different.

This time. . .

Pointing the remote control at the TV, Alec flipped it off. He hadn't kissed Lydia tonight, but he'd sure wanted to. They'd spent a long time gazing into each other's eyes at her front door before he took his leave, and now he felt like some lovesick schoolboy. It'd happened just this way with Denise, too. He'd fallen fast, and he'd fallen hard. And now Lydia.

Lord, You're going to have to take over here, 'cause I'm scared. Real scared. And Lydia and I have another date tomorrow night—except I just might die if I have to wait that long to see her again.

Standing, Alec turned off the lamp on the end table beside the sofa and walked into his bedroom. Maybe if he had a good night's sleep he'd wake up thinking straight in the morning.

Yeah, that's it. A good night's sleep.

ten

Alec made it until eleven o'clock before he couldn't stand it anymore and decided to trek over to Lydia's house. Thinking he needed an excuse, he wheeled the bike he'd given Tyler alongside him. The day was damp and gloomy, but the rain had stopped, and Alec thought if the kid played his cards right, his mother might even allow him to take back his new bike.

Walking up the driveway, he paused outside the back door and knocked loudly. Tyler answered.

"Hi, Mr. Alec."

"Hi. Is your mom busy?"

"No. I'll get her."

He turned and Alec watched through the screen door as the boy ran back into the kitchen, calling for her. Within minutes, Lydia strode toward him, wearing a pink wool sweater with an off-white turtleneck underneath it, a denim split skirt, and thick, ivory socks tucked snugly into brown, leather ankle boots.

"Hi." She opened the door and beckoned him into the hallway.

He smiled. "Expecting the temperature to fall to fifty below?" he asked amusedly.

She frowned, puzzled, and Alec chuckled.

"Your outfit, Lydia. You look like someone who lives in the North Pole."

"Excuse me," she said in feigned haughtiness, "but I'm freezing."

"It's warm out here."

"Oh, it is not. You're just a thick-blooded Northerner."

Throwing his head back, Alec hooted.

Lydia gave him a quelling look, smiling all the while, and then Alec spotted Tyler standing a short distance away, watching them curiously.

"I, um, brought the bike back," he said earnestly now. "That is, if it's okay with you."

Lydia turned and eyed her son before bringing her gaze back to his, and Alec realized for the first time just what a petite, little thing she really was, standing no taller than his shoulders.

"Tyler has a bike," she began. "He doesn't really need another. I've been trying to teach both my children the difference between wanting something and needing it."

"That's a good lesson," Alec replied carefully, trying to ignore the way the boy's face fell with disappointment. "But he'll probably outgrow the bike he's got soon enough and then he'll *need* a new one. Might as well keep this one. It's free."

"Yeah, Mama. Otherwise, it'll cost you money."

Lydia glanced at her son before her dusky blue eyes swung back around, searching Alec's face. The tiny tug at the corner of her mouth let him know she found his and Tyler's persuasiveness somewhat comical.

He grinned back at her. "Come on, Lydia," he said softly, "it's just a bike." Then, before he could think better of it, he reached out and brushed a strand of chestnut-colored hair from her cheek. A moment's look of surprise and something else—something unidentifiable—flittered across her lovely features before she blinked, obviously regaining her composure.

"That's right. It's just a bike," she repeated.

"Say yes, Mama," Tyler begged. "Please, say yes."

"Oh, well, I guess it can't hurt," Lydia agreed at last.

"Yippee!"

"But there's one condition," Alec declared above Tyler's cheering. He narrowed his gaze at Lydia. "You can't give the thing back—even if you get mad at me again."

She blushed, her cheeks matching the color of her sweater, and Alec felt thoroughly charmed.

"Can I go outside and ride it for a while?" Tyler asked.

Lydia nodded. "Yes, but put on a jacket."

"Aw, do I hafta? Mr. Alec said it's warm."

"Not warm enough for you. Jacket on."

Alec regarded her with interest as she gave her son one of those expressions only a mother could impart. He laughed softly under his breath.

"Yes, ma'am," Tyler muttered.

Lydia turned back to Alec. "Would you like to come in for a cup of coffee?"

"Sure."

As Tyler rushed out of the back door, Alec followed Lydia into the kitchen. She invited him to sit down at the table and he recognized the fancy, rose tablecloth that he'd first seen last week. Then Brooke entered the kitchen, asking if she could go outside and play, too.

"Yes, but stay in the backyard."

The little girl nodded.

"How do you like your coffee, Alec?"

"Black."

Lydia fixed up two cups before claiming a seat beside him at the table.

"So did you say you've lived in North Carolina all your life?" Alec asked, taking a swallow of his brew.

"Yes. I was born in a small city near the coast, but after my father died, my mother moved us to Charlotte."

"Brothers? Sisters?"

"Neither. Just me. What about you?"

"Two older sisters. I'm the baby of the family."

Lydia grinned. "You're an awfully big baby," she drawled teasingly.

"Yeah, well, what can I say?" Alec chuckled and a few moments of silence passed. "So, does your mother still live around here?"

"Yes. She's in Charlotte, but now lives with her new husband. She and Pete were married about nine months ago."

"Interesting." Alec took another drink. "My folks are divorced, but neither remarried. I guess the first time around was enough for both of them."

"What about you?" Lydia asked. "You talked about a broken engagement at the Bible study. . . ."

"Yep. And there's not much to tell, other than Denise—that was her name—up and changed her mind about marrying me."

"I'm so sorry."

Alec shrugged. "Nothing to be sorry about, really. Can I ask you something personal?"

"I suppose. . .but how personal?"

Alec laughed. "What's your middle name?"

Lydia paused, as if momentarily taken aback. "My middle name? It's Rose. Why do you ask?"

"Just wondering. I've been trying to imagine what it'd be. I thought maybe Ann or Marie. But Rose fits you just perfect. Lydia Rose, Southern belle."

"Oh, hush," she quipped, blushing profusely. "And what's your middle name?"

"Guess."

Lydia rolled her eyes, but sat thinking it over. Alec watched her pretty mouth trying different names on her tongue. Finally she picked one. "James."

"Right."

"Really? And here I'm not very good at guessing games." Laughing softly, she stood and walked to the counter with her cup. "Would you care for more coffee?"

"Sure would."

Lydia refilled his cup once, then again, and finally three times before their coffee klatch came to an end two hours later. After Alec left the house, she took the cups to the sink. Pulling out the bread and the peanut butter and jelly jars, she made sandwiches for Tyler and Brooke, who were no doubt ready to dash inside any minute for lunch. Before she finished, the door banged shut behind her predictable pair.

"Mama, you like him more and more, don't you?" Ty asked perceptively, noisily sitting down and scraping the chair closer to the table.

"Yes, I do."

"And he likes you, too."

"I think he does."

"Oh, he does," Brooke said adamantly, nodding her blond head as though she were an expert on such matters.

Lydia just smiled and began wiping off the counter. Yes, they liked each other—enough to pursue this relationship further. The thought sent a stream of delight mingled with apprehension through her veins. Gerald wouldn't like him—somehow she just knew it.

She and Alec had discussed a wide gamut of subjects this morning, and Lydia ended up divulging the details surrounding her mother and the church discipline issue. Alec had said the disciplinary action didn't sound right to him, since Pete professed to be a Christian. "Sounds to me like your father-in-law was standing in judgment of the guy. But, Lydia, I'm no authority on the subject. I'd have to research the topic of church discipline in the Bible."

Lydia nibbled her lower lip in contemplation. *It didn't sound right to Alec.* He'd given her his objective opinion, putting the question in her own heart. And now more than ever, Lydia wanted to phone her mother. Glancing out the window, she realized it had started raining again.

"Can me 'n' Brooke watch a movie?" Tyler asked. "What about the one Gramma bought us?"

"Yes, that's fine."

The children left the table and headed for the den. Standing with her back to the kitchen sink, Lydia watched them go before she eyed the phone on the wall. *Should I call?*

Lord, if I'm wrong to do this, then I deserve to be found out. If going against Gerald's wishes is going against Your will, I'll suffer the consequences. She collected her address book from the drawer at the end of the counter where she kept the phone books. *But if my mother's church discipline wasn't fair—if it wasn't right—I trust You will protect me from suffering a similar reproof.* Picking up the phone, Lydia dialed her mother's number.

eleven

Mesmerized, Alec watched Lydia gracefully move around her living room in a winter-white tea-length jacket-dress accented with red satin embroidery on the bodice and along the skirt's hem. He thought the outfit hugged her form, but in a modest way, and in a fashion that offered Lydia a certain elegance and grace. He felt like the luckiest guy in the world, taking her out tonight.

"All right now, you two behave yourselves," she drawled, kissing Brooke, then Tyler before giving the baby-sitter a final word of instruction. The sitter, an older woman with a grand-motherly disposition, had been introduced to Alec as Lydia's next-door neighbor on the other side—Mrs. Connie Wilberson.

"We'll be just fine, honey," the matronly woman insisted, her stocky frame perched on one end of the sofa. "You and Mr. Alec have a nice time." She grinned like a cat, looking from one to the other. "Did Pastor Boswick set up this match?"

"No, he didn't," Lydia replied vaguely.

"Oh?" The gray-haired woman's round face contorted with concern.

"Not to fret, Mrs. Wilberson, my father-in-law has met Alec." Lydia turned toward him. "Isn't that right? You two met the Sunday after you moved in."

"That's true." Alec thought Lydia looked a bit nervous, and he wondered, again, if they were making a mistake. Maybe they should put a stop to this relationship before it went any further. Maybe—

No, I prayed about this and decided to trust the Lord to guide my steps, Alec reminded himself. *I'm not going to wimp out now.*

"Alec, I think we'd best go before we're late."

He snapped to attention. "Right."

Lydia snatched her coat and purse and they headed for the door.

"Bye, Mr. Alec!" Ty called.

"Bye, kid."

Brooke waved shyly and smiled. Mrs. Wilberson appeared glued to her post, unanswered questions pooling in her eyes.

Outside, Alec helped Lydia into his truck. Before closing the door, he propped a palm against the frame and peered at her. "You're not obligated to come with me tonight, Lydia. I mean, if you don't think it's a good idea or that your father-in-law might not approve. . ."

"But I want to go out with you tonight," she replied softly, causing Alec's heart to flip inside his chest. "And for the record, my father-in-law does not make my decisions."

Alec grinned. "Okay, lady. I gave you one last chance to back out." Closing the door, he laughingly walked around to the driver's side and climbed in. *So, Lydia has some spunk after all.* He strapped on his seatbelt and glanced at her. "By the way, you look like a million bucks tonight."

"Only a million?" Lydia retorted.

Starting the engine, he chuckled and backed out of the driveway. The night definitely held promise. "I can tell we're going to have a good time."

She returned his smile.

"Except," Alec added, shifting gears as he drove down the street, "I never imagined a Southern belle like you would have even an ounce of gumption in your veins. I thought you were a docile little thing."

"Disappointed?" she asked carefully.

"No. Just surprised."

"I imagine it's my mother's fault," she drawled. "I called her this afternoon and obviously some of her *rebellion* rubbed off on me."

"I sincerely hope you're kidding, Lydia," Alec said, seriously now. "I mean, following your heart and marrying a Christian man, like you said your mom did, isn't rebellion in my book—God's either, as far as I know."

"And it's not as though my mother is a teenager who thwarted parental authority."

"That's right." He momentarily looked her way. "So, were you kidding just now or what?"

"Yes, I was being sarcastic. I apologize."

"No need. But I guess I never saw your sense of humor in action before either. And, no, I'm not disappointed. I like it."

Lydia glanced his way, wearing a slip of a grin. "May I share something very personal with you?"

"Sure, as long as it's not going to get me arrested or anything."

She laughed. "Hardly."

"Okay, go for it."

Her voice quickly became soft and solemn. "I'm realizing that after Michael died, part of me went dormant. But now I feel like I'm awakening to life again."

"Oh, yeah?" Alec saw her nod.

"And I think it all began when you moved in next door."

"Hmm. . ." He wasn't sure how to respond. He felt flattered, more than flattered. He was both glad and relieved she felt the same way he did, but this thing between them was happening too fast. Wasn't it? "Look, Lydia—"

"I know. Don't say it."

"Say what?"

"That you're not ready for a commitment, we barely know each other, that we're only on our first date. I'm aware of the facts. And the last thing I want to do is push you in any one direction. But, just the same, what I told you is the truth. I can't help it."

"Aw, I'll bet you say that to all the guys," he teased her, suddenly uncomfortable with the perilous turn to their conversation.

Lydia rapped him in the arm with her purse and Alec chuckled. But she didn't say another word about their relationship during the remainder of the trip to the restaurant. Oddly, he couldn't figure out if that made him feel better or worse.

When at last they arrived, he walked around his vehicle to assist Lydia. "I never rode in a pickup truck before," she told him when her feet touched the pavement.

"Used to Lincolns, eh?"

"Oh, please, don't remind me about that ill-fated night with Sim." She clucked her tongue.

Smiling, Alec threw caution to the wind and took her hand as they walked through the parking lot. The Valentine's Day dinner party was held in one of the banquet rooms of the Southern Cross Restaurant, which overflowed with a laughing, chatting throng of people. They squeezed their way through the queue of smartly dressed men and women, waiting for vacant tables, and found the Heritage Craft Furniture group standing around, mingling.

"Don't look now, Lydia," Alec leaned over and whispered loudly, "but Greg Nivens is about to drop his teeth."

"What?" Lydia frowned in confusion.

"Greg Nivens," he explained, his hand still enveloping hers, "is my supervisor. He also attends your church, and I think he's surprised to see you here. No, make that *shocked*. The guy is definitely shocked."

"Greg Nivens?" Lydia repeated the name. "I don't believe I know him. But then, again, ours is such a large church. It's impossible to know everybody."

"Well, here he comes, so you'll get a chance to meet him now. And I think that's his wife with him."

Lydia followed the direction of Alec's gaze and spotted the attractive pair heading their way. Having faces to put with the name, she recognized them at once. Still, when the Nivenses reached them, introductions were made.

"We know Mrs. Boswick," Greg said, rocking on his heels. "Doesn't everyone at SPCC?"

Lydia gave the man a polite smile. He was the proverbial

tall, dark, and handsome type right down to the dimple in his left cheek, and suddenly she recalled Michael's term for men at SPCC—*plastic people.*

Alec released Lydia's hand, turning her way. "Want a pop or something? I'll go get you one."

"Mineral water would be nice."

"Coming right up."

Lydia watched him walk away before giving her attention back to the Nivenses.

"Small world, isn't it?" Greg said curiously.

"Yes, sir, it is."

"How'd you meet up with Alec, anyway? He just moved to town."

"He's my next-door neighbor."

"Ahh. . . ," the couple said simultaneously, as though they'd just figured out one of the great mysteries of the world.

"Guess he works fast, too, eh?" Greg replied slyly, laughing at his own comment.

Lydia forced a smile.

"Okay, now, be honest," he said amusedly as he leaned slightly forward. "Does the pastor know you're out with my newest employee?"

"Why do you ask?"

"Well, it's just that Pastor Boswick seems awful particular about who his family associates with."

"He is, but Alec is a fine man."

"I agree. And he's a hard worker. I just meant. . .well, he's not one of *us.*"

"A member of SPCC?"

"That's right."

"Well, now, perhaps Mrs. Boswick will be the one to persuade him to apply for membership," Greg's wife suggested, patting the side of her French twist. "You know how convincing those Boswicks are." She smiled indulgently.

Greg agreed. "But I don't need convincing when it comes to our pastor's innocence, and I want you to know that my wife and I are behind your family all the way."

"Why, thank you." When Greg looked like he might enjoy continuing their discussion about the scandal, Lydia sought a quick escape. "I'd better go see if Alec needs some help. Excuse me." She hurried toward Alec, just as he finished getting their mineral water.

"People are really putting away the booze here tonight," Alec remarked, handing Lydia one of the glasses in his hands. "But I shouldn't be surprised. Before I knew the Lord, I drank like a fish myself."

She smiled. "You have the funniest sayings. 'Dropped his teeth.' 'Drank like a fish. . .' "

"I'm glad you find me so entertaining."

Several of Alec's buddies approached them and Lydia was introduced to more people. The evening progressed and dinner was served. She discretely observed Alec's table manners and felt mildly impressed—he selected the correct fork for his salad, even going so far as to pick up his knife and cut some of the larger leafy greens on his plate. He didn't talk with his mouth full, and he made good use of his napkin. Lydia wondered if perhaps his mother played "restaurant" with him like she did with her children. Regardless, he'd picked up proper social etiquette somewhere along the line.

In between dinner and dessert, Alec sat back and stretched his arm over the top of her chair. At the same time, she caught sight of the Nivenses sitting two tables away, staring in her direction. No doubt they disapproved of her being there with Alec. Gerald wouldn't approve of her dating him, either; however, Lydia hoped to get around him somehow. How exactly, she wasn't sure. But she planned to be firm about her decision to see Alec—even if it meant standing up to Gerald, something she wanted to avoid. He'd done so much for her in the past, but did she owe him her life in return? According to her mother, yes. Gerald would expect that and nothing less.

"I had always thought Southern Pride Community Church was a wonderful place to worship God and fellowship with other believers," her mother had stated during their conversation that afternoon. "I had the utmost respect for Gerald, but he'd been using me—and my money—all along. He's using you, too, honey."

Although the statement worried her, Lydia wanted to shrug off what her mother said as sheer ridiculousness. Using her? Hardly. Gerald had been a bulwark in Lydia's life since Michael died. And yet, in her heart of hearts rang a warning knell. Could the extortion allegations be true? And if such problems were really rippling through SPCC, why hadn't she taken notice of them? Were they that imperceptible as her mother claimed, or had she been totally blind to the facts? It was true—while in her hibernation of grief, Lydia hadn't been able to see beyond her everyday duties, caring for her children, working at her job. Now, however, it seemed she was awakening to a veritable nightmare!

☙

"I don't know why I'm telling you all this," Alec said much later as they sat in his truck, parked in Lydia's driveway. "Your baby-sitter is probably anxious to get home."

Lydia shook her head. "Mrs. Wilberson always falls asleep. It's all right. Besides, I'm glad you told me about Denise. It helps me get to know you. Except. . ." She paused and, under the glow of the full moon, Alec saw her thoughtful expression. "I can't understand why that woman up and changed her mind."

"Me, neither."

"Does it still hurt?"

Lydia's velvet drawl was like a soothing salve, but he'd be a liar if he said the pain of being dumped had completely gone. "A little," he finally replied. "It still hurts a little."

A long paused settled between them.

"Well, we should get you inside before you catch a night chill," Alec announced facetiously. "You Southern belles aren't used to these frigid temperatures."

"Ooh! You can say that again!" As if to emphasize it, she shivered.

Unable to contain his laughter, he climbed out of his truck and walked around to the other side. Lydia hadn't budged, but waited for him to open the door and help her down. And a good thing he noticed, too, or he'd look pretty stupid walking to the porch all by himself. *Denise usually beat me out of the truck. I never held the door for her.*

Together he and Lydia walked to her front door, and Alec recalled her conversation with Sim about kissing on the first date. Whether it was pure arrogance or a good case of male ego, Alec couldn't be sure, but he knew he was going to get a kiss out of Lydia tonight or die trying.

"Thanks a lot for coming to the party with me," he began.

She smiled. "It was fun—and I mean it."

He grinned and watched her dig in her purse for her house keys. Clasping them in her palm, she looked back at him.

"Good night."

" 'Night, Lydia."

In two smooth, practiced moves, Alec stepped forward and gathered her into his arms, pausing only briefly to view her reaction. When she didn't protest, he lowered his mouth to hers. But the moment their lips met, Alec knew he'd made a grave error.

He cut the kiss short. "I better go."

Lydia nodded. Was that disappointment he saw in her eyes?

"See ya," he said hastily.

"Good night," she replied once more.

Back in his truck and leaving her driveway, Alec berated himself for being such a fool. Oh, he'd won the challenge and gotten the prize, but he hadn't considered the consequences, and they were steep. Having tasted Lydia's sweet kiss tonight cost him plenty.

It had just cost Alec Corbett his very heart.

twelve

As Lydia fed her children a snack the following evening, she threw a glance next door. She hadn't seen Alec all day, even though she'd hoped to run into him after church that morning and invite him over for lunch—since it was Valentine's Day. But then as now, his house looked dark and deserted.

"Mama?" Tyler's voice penetrated her thoughts and Lydia gave him her full attention. "Matt's E-mail address doesn't work."

"Yes, I figured."

"Could I call him? I won't talk long."

"I don't know. . . ."

"I got his phone number from his aunt Rita. I saw her at church tonight."

Lydia hesitated, but only because she wasn't sure how welcomed Ty's call would be. Then again, he and Matt had stayed true-blue companions even though she and Sherry's friendship had come to an abrupt halt. "All right," she acquiesced. "I suppose you can phone Matt."

His mouth full of cheese and crackers, Tyler jumped off his chair and ran for the phone hanging on the wall on the other side of the kitchen.

"Chew your food before placing the call."

The boy swallowed. "Okay." He pulled a slip of paper from his pants pocket, picked up the receiver, and dialed the number. After a few moments, he smiled. "Hello, this is Tyler. Can Matt talk?"

Lydia listened quietly as she straightened up the kitchen.

"Mama?" Brooke asked, still sitting at the table. "Could I have a friend from school come over and play?"

"I think so," Lydia replied, sensing that her daughter

missed the Smiths' little girl, Pamela, even though she was a year older than Brooke. "Maybe next weekend."

"Goodie!" Brooke exclaimed before nibbling on another cracker.

"Yeah, and a man moved next door named Mr. Alec," Tyler was saying. "He's really big, and he doesn't even care if me 'n' Brooke stand on the fence. And guess what else? He and my mom went on a date last night!"

"Oh, Ty, I don't think Matt cares about that," Lydia remarked softly, feeling oddly embarrassed.

"I think they're gonna get married."

"Tyler!" This time Lydia's voice carried throughout the entire room.

"It's true, Mama," the boy replied with the receiver under his chin and an earnest expression on his face. "I knew it from the first day I saw Mr. Alec moving in. Isn't that right, Brooke?"

She nodded. "We thought you'd like him, Mama."

Lydia sighed. "My two children, Woodruff's own matchmakers!" After rolling her eyes, she tapered her gaze at Tyler. "Hurry up and finish your call, now. Long distance is expensive."

"Yes, ma'am. What did you say, Matt? Oh, yeah."

Tyler began disclosing various events at school while Lydia instructed Brooke to go upstairs and change into her nightie.

"Mama? Mrs. Smith wants to talk to you now," Tyler announced, following several minutes of idle chitchat with Matt.

Lydia was taken aback. Sherry? Wanted to talk to *her*? Slowly, she stepped to the phone and took the proffered receiver.

"Hello?" she said cautiously.

"Lydia? I know you probably loathe and despise me, but—"

"What are you talking about?"

A pause.

"I'm talking about Jordan and me and our public statement about Gerald."

"Oh, that." With one hand holding the phone to her ear, Lydia rubbed a troubled hand across her forehead. Why would Sherry even care what she thought? They hadn't spoken in months! And although Lydia still felt hurt and mourned the loss of their friendship, she wasn't angry, and she certainly didn't "despise" Sherry.

"May I explain?" Sherry asked.

"You don't have to. . . ."

"Yes, I do. I want you to understand. I want to. . .apologize. There's so much you don't know."

Lydia stretched the phone cord out and grabbed a kitchen chair. Lowering herself into it, she waved Tyler upstairs so he couldn't eavesdrop.

"It started last November," Sherry began softly. "Jordan, being the treasurer at SPCC, noticed some things about the books that made him uncomfortable. For instance, Gerald had withdrawn an awful lot of money for that new car he drives. Now, while SPCC agreed to furnish its pastor with an automobile, Jordan never expected him to choose a BMW 750iL—the thing cost nearly seventy thousand dollars! I mean, really!" Sherry declared. "What's wrong with a twenty thousand dollar Ford or Chevrolet?"

"I didn't realize the church paid for Gerald's car," Lydia stated lamely.

"His car *and* his house," Sherry added emphatically. "When the congregation agreed to purchase a home for SPCC's paster, they weren't thinking of the half a million dollar mansion he chose. What does an older couple nearing retirement need with seven bedrooms, a swimming pool, Jacuzzi, and tennis courts when there are needy families at SPCC?"

Sherry paused and Lydia sensed she was gathering steam. "When Jordan suspected a misuse of funds, he approached Gerald with his concerns and that's when your father-in-law threw a fit. He called Jordan a backslider for having the audacity to question his motives. Next, Gerald removed him from his treasurer's position, only to replace him with Sim Crenshaw."

"Oh, Sherry, I don't know what to think anymore," Lydia lamented. "I'm so confused over all of this."

"I'm sure you are. When Jordan told me everything, I had a hard time coming to grips with the truth myself."

Lydia shook her head, trying to clear it. Her thoughts were as boggled as this whole ordeal. "Why didn't you say something to me sooner?" she couldn't help asking Sherry. "Why did you end our friendship?"

"I didn't want to," she replied, sounding contrite. "But Jordan and I were scared Gerald would retaliate somehow, so we laid low for a while until Jordan got his new managerial position here in Tennessee. Then we moved. But now we see how wrong we were to run away from the situation instead of braving it out and trusting the Lord to see us through. That's why I need to apologize to you." She paused, her voice breaking slightly. "I'm so sorry and I've missed you so much!"

Lydia was trying to swallow her own onslaught of emotion. "I've missed you, too."

Sherry sniffed. "And I've been so worried about you. Gerald's been planning a match between you and Sim. Are you even aware of it?"

"Yes, I've gotten that impression."

"Honestly, Lyd," Sherry continued, using the pet name she'd coined for her years ago, "the very idea nauseates me. I know you trust Gerald completely, but don't be persuaded to marry Sim no matter how wonderful the promises sound. Simeon Crenshaw cannot be trusted."

"Don't worry. I'm not interested in Sim."

"Good. You put my mind at ease. Well, I have more to say to you, but we've talked plenty long on your bill. Let me call you right back and we can chat some more."

"I'd like that. . .but wait about a half hour so I can get Ty and Brooke into bed. Okay?"

Sherry agreed, they hung up, and Lydia took to the stairs, climbing them two at a time. She felt a bit of remorse for making such quick work of tucking her children in for the night, but she didn't want to miss Sherry's call. So many questions suddenly had answers, although Lydia couldn't say she cared for any of them. And it seemed she was caught in some sort of double bind, for if she chose to believe her mother and Sherry, then she'd have to conclude Gerald wasn't the godly, benevolent pastor she'd thought.

Oh, Lord, I'm so confused right now.

Walking into the den, Lydia grabbed the cordless phone and made her way into the living room. She sat down on the couch just as it rang. *Sherry always had uncanny timing.* Chuckling softly, she pressed the TALK button.

"My, but you're prompt," she answered.

"Lydia?" a male voice said.

She swallowed her amusement. "Gerald. Hello."

"Hello. Obviously you weren't expecting my call."

"No, I. . .I thought you were someone else. But how are you? Have you talked to Elberta?"

"I'm fine and I spoke with Elberta not long ago. She's decided to spend the rest of the winter in Florida with Mary."

"I see." Lydia felt troubled by the news. Was this some kind of separation, the first step toward divorce?

"Now I have a question for you. What's this I hear about you carrying on with your next-door neighbor?"

Lydia almost choked on her reply. "Who told you that? Mrs. Wilberson?"

"It doesn't matter. I want the truth, Lydia."

"I'm hardly 'carrying on' with him," she stated in her own defense. "We had a date last night and he kissed me good night. That's it."

"Hmm. . .that's more than Sim got, from what I understand."

"That's because I don't like Sim," Lydia stated tersely. She wished she'd realized sooner that her father-in-law had been bent on a match between them. It just wasn't going to happen.

"Am I to assume you *like* your neighbor? What's his name? Alex?"

"Alec. Alec Corbett. And, yes. . . ," she paused, sending up a quick arrow of a prayer for understanding, "yes, I like him. Very much."

"Very much?" he repeated as if he couldn't quite grasp the concept. Then a long pause passed between them before Gerald spoke up again. "Lydia, I thought we had an agreement. I was to screen prospective suitors for you."

"Yes, but I only went along with it because I wasn't capable of such a decision on my own so soon after Michael died. I couldn't think of dating. But it's different now."

"And why's that?"

She shrugged, forgetting her father-in-law couldn't see the gesture. "I don't know. It's as if the fog that hung over me has finally lifted."

"And we have *Alex* to thank for this, eh?"

"Alec." Lydia bristled under the condescension, but she fought to keep her temper in check. She'd known Gerald wouldn't approve of her seeing him, and yet this was the moment she'd hoped for—her shot at changing his mind. "Won't you please give him a chance?" she asked sweetly. "I think you'll like him. In some ways, Alec reminds me of Michael."

Gerald seemed to ignore the comment. "Is he a believer?"

"Yes."

"You're sure?"

"Positive."

"Where is he attending church?"

"At Berean Baptist."

"Oh, Lydia," her father-in-law ground out, sounding frustrated, "that's a Milquetoast church. If this man is a Christian— and I do mean *if*—he's probably a very weak one with no godly standards to speak of."

"On the contrary, I think he's a strong Christian. Please don't pass judgment on him before getting to know him first. I think you'll be surprised."

Another pause. "Very well. I didn't call to argue. I'm only

looking after your welfare. . .and that of the children."

"Thank you, but there's no need to be concerned."

"Well, of course there is! I'm Tyler and Brooke's grand-father. I have a vested interest in your love life."

The front doorbell suddenly chimed, startling Lydia from her thoughts. Standing she padded to the hallway, where she flipped on the porch light. Peeking out the side window, she saw Alec.

"Lydia? Are you still there?" Gerald sounded indignant.

"Yes, but I have to go. I'll talk to you soon. Bye." She clicked off the phone before setting it on the adjacent table. Then she pulled open the door and smiled.

"Happy Valentine's Day," Alec greeted her, placing a green tissue-wrapped bouquet in her arms. "Roses for Lydia Rose."

She felt her cheeks warm with a blush.

"Am I disturbing anything?"

"No. Would you care to come in?"

Alec shook his blond head. "Better not. After last night, I don't trust myself."

"What do you mean?"

A frown furrowed his thick, sandy-colored brows. "Lydia, at the risk of you freezing to death there in the doorway. . ." He smirked good-naturedly. "Want to go put on your winter coat, cap, and mittens? It's about fifty degrees out here and what I want to say might take awhile."

"I think I'll survive the frigid temperatures, Alec," she stated in jest. "What's on your mind?"

He leaned against the doorjamb. "Well, I've got to confess that in all the months I was engaged to Denise, I never kissed her. Do you believe that? It's true. You see, shortly after my conversion to Christ, I committed myself to the principles of courtship—no kissing, hugging, hand holding. . .any intimate physical contact, no matter how accepted it might be as far as worldly dating."

"I see."

"Are you sure?" Alec grinned, looking thoroughly amused.

"Most Christians haven't even heard of courtship."

"Well, I've heard of it. I just thought it went out with the antebellum South."

Alec hung his head back and hooted. "That's a good one, Lydia."

She shrugged, smiling, although she had to admit, she wasn't sure where Alec was going with all of this.

Then he pulled out several pamphlets from his inside jacket pocket and gave them to her. With the flowers cradled in one arm, Lydia accepted them with her other hand.

"I talked to Pastor Spencer tonight after church," Alec continued. "He promotes courtship and he managed to dig up some literature on the subject. I'd like you to read those brochures. They'll explain everything a lot better than I can."

"I'll read them tonight."

"Great. I wrote down my cell phone and home phone numbers. Call me if you have any questions. And I apologize for kissing you last night. I violated my own code of ethics."

Lydia nodded, but inside, her heart was breaking. "Alec, I think you're politely trying to tell me you don't want to see me anymore."

His topaz-colored eyes widened in shock. "No way, quite the opposite. But you're the one who said you weren't interested in remarrying. See, Lydia, that's a problem since courtship is a forerunner to marriage. Courtship isn't another word for dating. It's completely different." He gave her a sympathetic smile. "Will you just read those brochures?"

"Yes. . .yes, I will. Now I'm curious."

"Good. And, um, just one more thing. . . ."

Lydia raised her brows expectantly.

"I want you to know this is no light matter with me. I left Wisconsin determined not to get involved with another woman as long as I lived. After we met, I wanted to stay as far away from you, Lydia, as I could get. . .because I felt an immediate attraction to you. And, honestly, I'm not a man who's easily swayed by a pretty face. I've seen enough of them to know better. I became a Christian when I was thirty years old and I didn't exactly live a priestly existence. But, praise the Lord, He saved me before I could really mess up my life."

Lydia smiled, touched that Alec would share something so personal. His sensitivity was showing again, his vulnerability on display, and she could see why he was hurt so deeply over his broken engagement. Once more, that particular feeling came over her, the one that caused her to want to be the woman who changed Alec Corbett's heart about love and marriage.

"Lydia, at the risk of sounding like a complete lunatic," Alec said with a wry grin, "I want to—well, that is, if you want me to—I mean, I know we've only known each other a couple of weeks and everything, but. . ."

She sucked her lower lip between her teeth to keep from smiling. He looked so cute standing there, rambling on nervously.

"What I'm trying to say is, I'd like to court you."

"I'm flattered, and I—"

"Read those pamphlets before you answer, okay? But if you have reservations or doubts of any kind, I understand. Like I said, we've only known each other a short time. It's just that. . .well, I could fall in love with you real easy. . .if I haven't already."

"Oh, Alec. . ." Lydia was touched to the heart.

"You go on in the house now, before you turn into an icicle, and I'm going home before I do something we both might regret. I was wrong to be so careless last night. Guess I haven't been walking as close to the Lord as I should. But I want to make things right from tonight on, okay?"

She nodded and, watching him go, she felt more impressed with Alec than ever. In her mind, he was a gentleman among gentlemen.

The phone rang again, and she reentered the hallway, closing the door and latching it securely behind her. Picking up the cordless, she smiled, hearing Sherry's voice.

"Okay, Lyd, kids are asleep and we can catch up. . .it's about time, wouldn't you say?"

"Oh, I'd say, all right. And, Sherry, I've got to tell you about my new next-door neighbor. You're not going to believe this. . .I think I'm in love!"

&

"You fool. He's done in two short weeks what you've been trying to do for over a year!" Gerald paced the hardwood floor of his mountain cabin while Sim sat comfortably in a nearby armchair.

"It's not over yet. I've still got a couple of tricks up my sleeve."

"There's no time for tricks," Gerald spat irritably. "Lydia is positively smitten."

"She won't be for long." Sim grinned conspiratorially, rose from the chair, and walked to his briefcase, lifting out a folded document. "I hired an investigator who ran a check on our friend, Mr. Alec Corbett. Take a look."

Gerald felt hopeful for the first time in days.

"He's got a past a mile long."

Reading over the report, Gerald smiled. "Very good. Very good." He glanced up at Sim. "You've done a fine job. When Lydia sees this, she'll be appalled." He pursed his lips in thought. "I'll return home tomorrow and confront her."

"No. Wait a week or so."

"What? And give Mr. Corbett another week at romancing Lydia?

Sim nodded. "Another week and she'll be all the more hurt when you spring the news of his jaded past on her. Emphasize the women, Gerald. Don't be afraid to break her heart. And then I'll come along, and—"

"And dry her tears," Gerald finished incisively. He mulled over the idea. "Yes, I think that'll work just fine."

"Let's hope so," Sim said crisply. "SPCC's future is depending on it."

thirteen

Alec lay awake in bed, unable to sleep. He glanced at the digital alarm clock/radio on his headboard. It read 1:00.

Man, I've got to get some shut-eye!

He thought ahead to the busy day he had planned at work, starting in just several short hours, and groaned. Turning over, he plumped his pillow. If he could quit thinking about Lydia, a good night's rest might still be achieved.

It had been at Pastor Spencer's suggestion that Alec decided to share his heart with her and now he couldn't help wondering if he'd turned her off completely. He thought she would have called, but she hadn't. What did that mean? She wasn't interested in him and his courtship convictions?

Well, better to alienate her now than have her change her mind later, he tried to convince himself.

He began to reflect on how different they were—Lydia, a pretty little Southern belle and he, a "Yankee." She seemed so dignified compared to him, and yet Alec never felt inferior with her—she didn't allow it. In fact, Lydia Boswick, with her sweet ways, made him feel more like a man than any other woman he'd ever known.

Suddenly visions of his older sisters flitted through Alec's head. They wouldn't like her. Pat and Sandy knew how to make most men cower with their loud, bossy temperaments. Small wonder they made such good supervisors in the two Wisconsin factories where they worked. They were in their elements, but if they ever came face-to-face with Lydia's femininity, those two would undoubtedly declare that she set the women's rights movement back a hundred years.

Alec grinned in the darkness of his bedroom. Perhaps that was where the attraction was—thwarting his two sisters at last! No. It was more than that, of course. . .and if he didn't quit thinking about Lydia, he'd be a basket case at work tomorrow.

Rolling over once more, he closed his eyes and, out of sheer will, Alec finally slept.

☙

All of Monday, Alec stayed busy. He'd been assigned to work on a kitchen remodeling project and spent a majority of his day tearing out the old cabinetry and preparing to install the new cupboards. When he arrived back at home, it was dark outside. Lights glowed from Lydia's house as he walked from the garage, and he debated whether to call her, but decided not to push. She had a decision to make and if she was waiting on the Lord, praying for His direction, Alec didn't want to intrude.

He showered and thought he heard the phone ring. But after he was out and dressed, he checked his voice mail and since there weren't any messages, he figured he'd imagined it.

He watched a football game, read his Bible, and went to sleep, too exhausted to fret over his lovely next-door neighbor another whole night long.

☙

Tuesday morning found Lydia sitting at her desk, flipping through the literature Alec had given her Sunday night. She'd read and reread each pamphlet and now saw the wisdom behind courtship's principles, even though she had first viewed them as bothersome rules. But the more she considered them, the more she realized they were guides that served as lines of protection. "There isn't a more powerful drive than the desire for intimacy," the author of one pamphlet wrote. "Likewise, anyone familiar with our culture knows that few things have brought more heartache and despair than misguided passion." Lydia certainly couldn't disagree with that statement. She'd known a couple of Christian friends back in high school who had fallen into such sin and now, being the secretary at church, she frequently observed people coming in for counseling sessions with Gerald because of the devastation in their lives caused by immorality.

Glancing at her wristwatch, Lydia realized it was past noon. She wondered if Alec got a lunch break. Should she try calling him? Deciding to chance it, she picked up the receiver of her desk phone and dialed the cellular number he'd written down on one of the brochures. The adjacent offices around her were silent. The assistant pastor and youth pastor were attending seminars in Raleigh and her father-in-law was still out of town. With the moment's privacy, Lydia hoped to get to talk to Alec.

His phone rang for the third time and she was tempted to hang up when suddenly it stopped.

"Yeah, Corbett, here."

She brought her chin back in surprise at the brusque greeting. "Alec?" she said hesitantly.

A pause. "Hang on a sec." She heard muffled voices and the whir of a drill or electric saw in the background. Then Alec came back on the line. "Sorry about that. I had to tell the guys I was taking a break."

"Is this a bad time?"

"Nope."

"Good." She felt oddly nervous. "I just wanted to tell you I read the information you gave me."

"And?"

"And, I agree with it. . .them. . .I mean, the courtship idea."

"Are you okay? You sound upset or something."

"Yes, I'm fine. I just feel like. . .like I'm an awkward sixteen-year-old again," Lydia admitted, twirling the phone cord around her index finger.

Alec laughed. "You, too, huh?"

She smiled.

"Well, maybe we can talk some more tonight. It's a nice day. How 'bout if I try to get off at a reasonable hour and we take the kids for ice cream?"

"I'm sure they'd love that, although I don't know how

much of a discussion we'll be able to have with Ty along."

"Guess we'll have to take our chances."

As much as Lydia loved her children, she felt a tad disappointed she couldn't have Alec's company all to herself. But the fact remained: If he entertained thoughts of marrying her someday, he would have to make a commitment to Tyler and Brooke also. It might be a good thing if he discovered just what he was in for at this early stage of their relationship.

"See you tonight, Lydia."

"Yes, see you tonight. . . ."

❧

The evening wind felt like a cold slap against Lydia's face as she sat in the park bleachers and watched Alec and Tyler throwing the football to each other. Having just indulged in a scoop of "Death by Chocolate" ice cream, she felt all the more chilled.

"Yea! Touchdown!" Brooke cheered beside her.

Lydia chuckled. She didn't think her daughter even knew what a touchdown was, but she seemed to be having a fun time clapping her hands and rooting for Tyler first and then "Mr. Alec." And Tyler was in his glory. Lydia hadn't seen her son so happy since last Christmas, when he got that computer from Gerald.

"Yea! Tyler caught the ball!" Brooke jumped up and down, applauding loudly, while Lydia shivered beneath her winter jacket.

At long last, Alec and Tyler walked off the field.

"Nice warm night for a football game, eh, Lydia?" Alec razzed with a mischievous gleam in his eyes.

"Very nice," she replied dryly, attempting to keep her teeth from chattering.

He chuckled as they all walked toward his pickup truck. Reaching it, Alec unlocked the door and Tyler and Brooke climbed into the backseat of the cab. Lydia slid into the passenger seat, glad to be out of the chilling wind.

"That was awesome!" Tyler exclaimed.

"Y'all are a good football player," Brooke drawled, complimenting her brother. "And I was a good cheerleader. Right, Mama?"

"That's right."

Alec opened the driver's door and seated himself behind the wheel. Turning the key in the ignition, the engine came to life and soon they were on their way home. Once they arrived, Lydia gave in and let the kids watch one of their favorite videos before bedtime.

"And I think I need some hot tea," she declared, rubbing her frozen hands together.

"I think I need an ice cold cola," Alec said, opening the fridge. "Mind if I help myself."

"Sure, go ahead. But all I've got in there is apple juice."

"You're kidding?" He closed the door, looking disappointed. "I think I'll go home."

"Oh, don't do that," Lydia said, feigning a pout.

He winked. "Okay, guess I'll come back after I grab a soft drink."

She chuckled lightly at Alec's retreating form and, in his absence, she set the kettle to boiling and steeped her tea. Pulling on a cozy sweater, she sat down at the kitchen table, listening to Tyler and Brooke giggling in the den. Minutes later, Alec walked through the back door.

"You know, your boy is starving for some male companionship," he announced, taking a seat opposite from Lydia's at the table. "I don't mean that as an insult. I know you're doing the best you can."

"But you're right. Ty needs a good male friend. He used to have Matt next door until the Smiths moved to Tennessee."

"Yeah, he told me about that." Alec took a few swallows from his can of cola. "He said something 'bad' happened."

"It did. And it involves my father-in-law and the extortion charges he's facing."

"Uh-oh." Alec twirled his pop can between his hands, studying it thoughtfully. "How are you coping with all of that?" he finally asked, bringing his gaze back to hers. "It's got to be stressful."

"It is and I'm a baffled mess," she admitted. "Sherry Smith was my very best friend and, even though Gerald wouldn't like it if he knew, I've had contact with her. We spoke on Sunday night. Hearing her version of why she and her husband left the church and ultimately North Carolina answered many of my questions. But it also raised some more." Lydia shook her head sadly. "I don't want to think badly of my father-in-law. He's been good to me and the children."

"Does he ever do anything special with Tyler? Man-to-man stuff, like taking him to a basketball game?"

Lydia shook her head. "He's too busy."

"Well, would you mind if I spent a little extra time with him? He can tag along with me when I shoot hoops with some of the guys from church. We try to get together a couple of times a month."

"Courting my son, too, are you?" Lydia teased.

Alec gave her a furtive glance. "Courting trouble's more like it."

"Who me?" she asked, batting her lashes innocently.

He smirked in reply and took another drink. "Speaking of trouble, I can foresee some obstacles ahead of us." His tone took on a serious note. "And your father-in-law is one of them."

"I talked to him on Sunday night, too, and I told him we went out the night before. . .well, actually he'd heard about it from someone at church." Lydia lifted the corners of her mouth in a slight grin. "News travels fast among SPCC's congregation."

"I guess. So did the good pastor blow a gasket?" Alec chuckled. "I mean, I am a *Northerner*, you know, and he was very quick to point that out when we were introduced."

"He's willing to give you a chance," Lydia said, praying it was so.

"And what if he doesn't approve?" he asked, wearing a

hardened expression. "Then it's off between you and me regardless of what we might feel the Lord is doing?" Alec pushed.

When Lydia hesitated, he scooted his chair back and stood. "Look, I think you need to get that matter settled first. Who are you listening to? God or your father-in-law?"

"God, of course," she replied, standing as well.

He gave her a skeptical look.

"Please, be patient with me," she whispered.

"I don't want to get hurt again," Alec said candidly. "So if you're going to change your mind, do it now."

"I'm not changing my mind. But at the same time, we need to stay open to the Lord's leading. What if He closes the door on this relationship?"

"If He does, it won't be for a political reason."

"I agree." She gazed at Alec, silently pleading with him for understanding.

"Obstacle number two," he touted in spite of her efforts. "Money. I'm a lowly carpenter, Lydia, and don't exactly make a fortune. Judging by this house and your lifestyle, you're accustomed to wealth."

"I didn't grow up with it. Mama wanted to save the insurance money Daddy left her for my college education and her retirement. I worked a part-time job all through high school while Mama cleaned houses for a living. We lived in a one-bedroom apartment and. . .we were very happy. As for my present situation, I know Michael left me some money, but my father-in-law is my agent. He takes care of everything. I get a monthly allotment, but I suspect the church is supporting me for the most part."

"You mean you don't know how much your husband left you?"

"I should, shouldn't I? But I'm afraid I was so distraught at the reading of Michael's will, that I don't recall the exact figures. And since Gerald so kindly agreed to take care of it all. . . ."

Alec shook his blond head. "This bothers me."

"Why?"

"Because your father-in-law could decide to pull your support if he doesn't approve and we continue to see each other." He tipped his head slightly. "Are you prepared for that, Lydia? What if you lose your financial security because of me?"

"That won't happen."

"Oh? Why won't it?"

"You're forgetting something. My children. Gerald would never allow them—or me—to suffer financial hardship if he could help it."

"Well, I've got news for you. You might suffer financial hardship with me—and I will not have anyone else supporting my family. I'll be the one to take care of my wife and kids." He paused, considering her earnestly. "You may have to choose between living in luxury in this grand house or living with me. And you might as well decide now and save us both a lot of grief."

"Can't I let God decide?" She smiled. "Actually, it's already been determined; all I have to do is let the Lord lead the way."

"Being less than wealthy doesn't scare you?"

"Not in the least."

"I'm warning you, Lydia, I won't ever accept financial help from your father-in-law or anyone else—not while I'm an able-bodied man and I can work."

She walked toward him. "I think you're wonderful."

"I think I'm crazy. You're out of my league, Lydia Rose Boswick."

"No, I am not 'out of your league,' and don't you ever say that again. You're a child of God and there are not *leagues* among Christians."

"You haven't been paying attention to your father-in-law's sermons, have you?" Alec asked facetiously before chuckling.

Lydia smiled, watching him and thinking his eyes fairly danced when he laughed like that. "I'm falling in love with you," she murmured helplessly.

"Yeah, well, I think I passed that point. So now you know

just what kind of fool you're dealing with." He smirked. "And on that note, I'd better say good night."

She watched him go in a mixture of disappointment and admiration. The kitchen had a lonely atmosphere about it after Alec left. Lydia stood there, staring at the closed back door. From the den, she could hear silly music playing on the video, but since Tyler and Brooke weren't laughing as usual, she guessed they'd fallen asleep.

On a long sigh, Lydia made her way into the den, thinking she'd met some kind of hero when Alec Corbett moved in next door.

fourteen

The rain fell in sheets as Alec stood in the doorway of Berean Baptist Church with his friend Larry after the midweek worship service.

"Okay, lemme get this straight," Larry said. "She loves you. You love her. . . ." He tipped his head. "What are you waiting for, stupid? Do you know how hard it is to find somebody to love in this world—somebody who loves you back?"

"Yeah, I know," Alec countered, "but I'd like to get to know her before I pop the question."

"You've got the rest of your lives to get to know each other." Larry seemed momentarily thoughtful—almost remorsefully so. "I entertained ideas of asking Lydia out, after that first night we were in her house for the Bible study."

Alec cut him a furtive glance. "Think again, buddy."

"Oh, I know. She's yours. But, to be honest, the fact that Lydia is a Boswick turned me off from the get-go. You I'd go up against 'cause you'd fight fair. But Gerald Boswick? Forget it."

"The guy's that bad, eh?"

Larry nodded and pulled his jacket collar closer around his neck. "His Holiness has a lot of clout around here. Knows people in high places. If he doesn't like you, he'll make your life miserable."

"Do you know that firsthand?"

"Somewhat. I know a guy who dared to stand up to Pastor Boswick with regards to Boswick wanting to erect that nice big church building he's got. This happened, oh. . .five years ago or so. There was a dispute between the pastor and SPCC's neighbors who didn't want a huge church on their corner and the crowd it would bring. Bill headed up the City Counsel and he sided with the townsfolk. Suddenly, his dog was found shot to death, and threatening phone calls were made to his wife during the day when Bill wasn't around. When he still refused to back down, Pastor Boswick allegedly called up one of his buddies over in Charlotte and, would you believe, Bill lost his job within a matter of hours? Next, there were a couple of mysterious fires at the homes of the neighboring opponents and so the others quickly shut their mouths. Of course, no one can actually *prove* it was Gerald Boswick's doing, although the fire marshal at that time was a member of SPCC."

"Wow." It was all Alec could think to say. And he had to admit, part of him felt leery about courting Lydia because of what he heard about her father-in-law. Except, the alternative didn't suit him either. Besides, God was bigger than Gerald Boswick, he reasoned.

"I have to admit," Larry added, "I still feel bad about getting rejected for membership at SPCC, but not because it was a good church and I wanted to sit under the teaching there. I'd been seeing a lovely, sweet lady named Maria. I sensed she might be the one for me. But when she got accepted into the fold and we no longer were 'equally yoked,' according to what Maria had been told, she broke things off with me. That was what really hurt. Worse, I see her around town sometimes. We had a special thing going, but now she won't even say hello to me."

"That's a bummer, all right." Alec pursed his lips thoughtfully. "Unequally yoked, huh? But that passage of Scripture warns believers not to join together with nonbelievers. It's not pegging Christians against each other."

"I know, but that's what they teach over there. If you aren't a member of SPCC, then you're not going to heaven—and those deacons, Pastor Boswick's own henchmen, are the ones deciding who's saved and who isn't."

"That's crazy."

"No kidding."

Alec took a moment to digest the information. "I don't think Lydia subscribes to that philosophy."

"Doesn't sound like it. Makes you wonder, though, how did

she, Pastor Boswick's daughter-in-law, make it to this point unscathed?"

"I think a lot of it had to do with her husband. Sounds like he was a pretty balanced guy. In fact, I spoke with our pastor and he said he had a lot of respect for Michael Boswick. Told me he was a 'good man.' "

"What did Mark say about Pastor Boswick? If you don't mind me asking." Larry grinned expectantly.

Alec smirked. "He said the guy scares him as much as the Ku Klux Klan."

"Whew! Well, buddy, I wish you a lot of luck," Larry said, clapping him on the back.

"Forget the luck," Alec retorted, "I need your prayers."

His friend sobered. "You got 'em, man."

❧

Gerald Boswick's office was never one Lydia enjoyed being inside. Oh, it had a pleasant enough decor from the warm blue-and-white scrolled wallpaper to the dark blue carpet covering the floor. The furniture was fashioned after a colonial style and offered adequate comfort. It wasn't the room, itself, Lydia minded. It was the ever-present sad memories that seemed to linger within its perimeters. How many times had she sat in this exact spot on the settee and wept over losing Michael, the situation with the Smiths, her mother. . .and now Alec.

"Lydia, I forbid you to see that man!" Gerald said, causing her to wish he hadn't come back from his mountain retreat.

"But you don't understand. I love him."

"That's ridiculous. He came to town three short weeks ago. You can't fall in love with someone in three weeks."

Lydia shrugged. "It happened."

With a derisive snort, he walked around his wide desk and sat on its edge. "What do you know of his background, his past? What kind of family does he come from?"

"I know he's got two older sisters," Lydia began, hating how insipid she sounded. "I know his parents divorced when Alec was young."

"A broken family?" An expression of disdain marred his features.

Lydia swallowed hard. "Many of today's godliest men have come from troubled homes, Gerald. You know that as well as I."

"But it's not been without consequence. Now, what else do you know about this neighbor of yours?"

"I know Alec became a born-again Christian at the age of thirty—he's thirty-five now."

Gerald folded his arms, hardly impressed. "Is that it?"

Was it? She searched her memory, thinking that surely she could come up with another fact or two. Finally, indignant over having to defend the man she loved, Lydia shook her head in aggravation. "He's a good man," she argued. "He wants to court me. When was the last time you heard of a man wanting to court a woman? Alec Corbett might be from Wisconsin, but he's got a manner about him that reminds me of an old-fashioned Southern gentleman."

"That tells me you know very little about him, my dear." Reaching across the desk, Gerald picked up a piece of paper. "Here's what a private investigator discovered."

Lydia stifled a gasp. "An investigator?"

"That's right." He glanced at the report in his hand. "Let's see. . .Alec Corbett was arrested not once, but twice. The first time it was for disorderly conduct, the second for driving under the influence."

"That had to be before he was saved."

"Regardless, it's a reflection on his character."

"No, it's the past. The Lord Jesus changed all that."

"Let me finish. Mr. Corbett has had three jobs in the last seven years—which spells instability. Furthermore, he's cohabited with three different women outside the bonds of marriage. The first in 1984, the second in 1987, and the third in 1992."

Lydia began to feel sick.

"That tells me he's unable to commit to a lasting relationship. In fact, he was engaged to be married to a woman named

Denise Lisinski. She broke it off just three short months ago."

"I know about Denise," Lydia muttered.

"Then you're aware of why she broke the engagement?"

"Yes. She changed her mind."

"Yes. . .but do you know *why*?"

Lydia looked up into her father-in-law's supremely satisfied face. "I have a feeling you're going to tell me."

He gave her a patient smile. "Miss Lisinski told the investigator that Alec Corbett frightened her with his bad temper. She called him extremely possessive and said he wouldn't allow her to see her friends." Handing the piece of paper to Lydia, he added, "Read it for yourself. It would seem he's got some psychological problems. I've seen the pattern before. Now, while he claims to know the Lord, I do not want him associated with my flock here at SPCC and I especially do not want him near my family. Think of the children, Lydia! Youngsters can rile even the most patient of men. What would happen if you married this veritable stranger and he lost his temper and hurt either Tyler or Brooke?"

"He'd never do that," she maintained, staring in disbelief at the sheet of paper in her hands. The typewritten words on the page were swimming before her rapidly filling eyes.

"You can do better than a man like Alec Corbett, my dear."

Wounded beyond imagination, she stood and slowly walked to the door, unwilling that Gerald should see her cry.

"I've got an idea," he said, halting her steps. Coming up behind her, he put his hands on her shoulders. "Why don't you and I go to your favorite restaurant in Charlotte this evening. We'll get someone to watch the children. . .my treat."

"No, thank you."

He gently, but firmly turned her around and peered into her face. "I know it hurts, dear. But he's not for you. Better to weep now and get him out of your system than marry him and live the rest of your life in utter misery."

"But—"

Gerald put a finger to her lips. "Shh. . .no more argument," he whispered, placing a kiss on her forehead. "Father knows best."

She nodded slightly and returned to her desk, where she fought down her emotions and tried desperately to concentrate on her work. She thought about phoning Alec and questioning him, but she didn't dare under her father-in-law's watchful gaze. Then Sim entered the office just before Tyler and Brooke were dismissed from school.

"Hello, Lydia," he greeted, sounding chipper. He paused at her desk, leaning sideways, one elbow resting on its surface. "You look down in the dumps today. Everything all right?"

"Just a bad day," she said, trying not to cry again.

"I'm sorry to hear that. What can I do to help?"

She shook her head. "Nothing, but thank you anyway."

"Lydia, you must know by now how much I care about you."

"I appreciate that, Sim, but—"

He walked around and entered her small work space. Kneeling by her chair, he took her hand. Lydia pulled away, glancing around the office nervously. She didn't want to be the subject of the latest gossip—especially not with Sim.

"I'm all right, really," she tried to assure him.

"Then I must tell you—I'm in love with you, my darling. I'll do anything to make you mine."

For the first time in hours, Lydia smiled. Sim's declaration sounded so melodramatic, it seemed funny.

She quickly swallowed her amusement, however, in order to be polite. "You're so kind to say that, but, I—"

"Name it and it's yours."

"Alec Corbett," she replied wistfully.

Sim frowned. "What?"

Lydia shook her head. "Never mind. It was a bad joke on my part. Forgive me." She stood and pushed her chair in under her desk. "Please excuse me, my children will be here shortly, and I've got to take them home."

Skirting her way around Sim, she left the office, leaving him there on his knees.

fifteen

With Tyler and Brooke in bed for the night, the house was very quiet. Too quiet. Shivering, more so from stress than from the cold March temperature or the rain outside, Lydia wandered from room to room, straightening this, tidying that, and all the while thinking about Alec and wondering. One glance next door told her he hadn't gotten home yet. He said sometimes he worked twelve- or fourteen-hour days Monday through Thursday and took Friday afternoons off. But obviously today wasn't one of those Fridays. Unless, of course, he had other plans she didn't know about.

Still feeling chilled, Lydia made a fire in the fireplace and sat down before it, watching the flames leaping upward. She felt convinced her father-in-law had told her the truth today, and she longed to ask Alec about the investigator's report, but she was scared. Suppose he was some kind of psychopath? What did she really know about him anyway?

Suddenly spying her Bible on the end table, Lydia felt a sudden longing for God's Word. *Speak to me, Lord. Show me the truth.*

She looked up her reading for the day: 2 Corinthians 5. She'd been too harried this morning for devotions. She began at verse seventeen. *"Therefore if any man be in Christ, he is a new creature: old things are passed away; behold, all things are become new."* On the lower half of the page, in the commentary portion of her Bible, Lydia continued to read that the apostle Paul literally meant those in Christ were God's new creations. Salvation brought on a changed lifestyle.

Lydia felt like laughing! It was no coincidence that *this* passage was part of her Scripture reading for *this* day. Just that small bit of God's Word had renewed her spirit.

She read through the rest of the chapter before reverently setting aside her Bible. She found the cordless phone and Alec's cellular number and placed the call.

"Corbett here."

"Hi, Alec. You must be working late tonight." Her casual air surprised even herself.

"Yep, but I'm just about home. We finished the project, the client is ecstatic, our whole crew gets a bonus. Guess the long hours were worth it." A pause. "Oh, hey. . .I didn't forget, did I? Were we supposed to go out tonight?"

"No." Lydia sighed, hating what had to come next. "Can you stop over? I have to talk to you. It's important."

"Sounds serious."

"It is."

"Hmm. . .can you give me a hint?"

Lydia paused to weigh the pros and cons—should she tell him or not? Finally, she decided to be direct. "My father-in-law hired an investigator who did a background check on you." When no immediate reply came forth, she wondered if they'd lost their connection. "Alec? Are you still there?"

"Yeah. I'm pulling into my driveway. Give me a half hour to clean up, okay?"

"Of course. . . ."

He'd hung up before she'd barely finished the last word.

Oh, Lord, I'm frightened. What if Alec does, indeed, have a nasty temper? What if he yells? What if he hates me for confronting him about his past?

As if in reply, she recalled a verse in 1 John 4: *"There is no fear in love; but perfect love casteth out fear."*

"For God hath not given us the spirit of fear," she said out loud, quoting one of her favorite promises from 2 Timothy, "but of power, and of love, and of a sound mind."

Lydia sat back down in her chair by the fire and prayerfully waited. Almost exactly thirty minutes later, the doorbell chimed. She swallowed nervously, but determined to let him have his say.

"Hi," she said, opening the door and bidding him entrance.

"Hi, yourself." He walked into the hallway. "Where do you want to talk?"

"Living room?"

With a nod, Alec strode across the room and made himself comfortable on the couch. Clad in a red-checked flannel shirt, he reminded Lydia of a big, blond lumberjack.

"Don't you ever wear a coat?" she couldn't help asking as she made her way toward him.

He seemed momentarily surprised by the question. "Who needs a coat? It's fifty-two degrees outside."

Giving him a hooded glance and a bit of a smile, she took the investigator's report off the coffee table and handed it to him. Then she sat on the opposite end of the couch while he read it over.

After a few minutes, he tossed it onto the cushion between them. He met her gaze, his expression revealing nothing. "What do you want me to say? It's all true."

"Alec, I've prayed about this and God reminded me that everyone in Christ is a new creature. Old things are passed away. But I wondered if you'd mind explaining."

"I don't mind, but it won't exactly be easy. I'm not proud of my past, Lydia. I try very hard to forget it. And I'm not sure where to start, so why don't you ask me some questions? What do want to know?"

She lifted the sheet of paper. "The disorderly conduct charge?"

"I was twenty-one and stupid. Got into a fight in a tavern over some woman."

"Driving while under the influence. . .?"

"Yep. I was drunk as a skunk. I'm just glad I didn't kill anyone. I think I was about twenty-five when that happened."

"And the women?" That of all things caused Lydia the most heartache.

"Did I read it correctly? There were three listed on that report?"

She nodded.

He scratched his jaw pensively. "I think there were more."

"Oh, Alec. . .you *think*?"

He shifted his weight, facing her directly. "Look, Lydia, I know my past is not pretty, but I'm a miracle of God's grace. Christ died for sinful men—for me! And maybe now you'll understand why I take courtship so seriously. While lost, I defiled myself, but I don't intend on sinning against my Savior."

She nodded. "Yes, I see your point clearly."

"But I can ease your mind by telling you I don't have any social diseases or HIV, and I haven't fathered any children."

"Well," she said, feeling a blush running up her neck at such a controversial topic of discussion. "I guess that's something." She fretted over her lower lip for several moments. "Alec, what about the things Denise said?"

Looking puzzled, he took the report and reread it. "I didn't see this the first time through," he murmured. Then glancing back at her, he added, "But I guess now I know why she broke off our engagement. She never would tell me. If she would have said something, we could have discussed it. And, yeah, I got mad at her—plenty of times. She liked to go to a downtown nightclub with her friends after work every Thursday night—Ladies' Night. Being a Christian woman, I didn't think it was right for her to be in such a place, but Denise said she was a witness to her unsaved girlfriends at work and that even Jesus ate with sinners. I was quick to remind her that our Lord ate at the homes of sinners. He never entered a den of iniquity, and that's what those nightclubs are. There's sensual rock music playing; the booze is flowing; and there's filthy men jeering at pretty women like Denise. I wanted her to stay out of there, but she wouldn't. So, I sort of laid down the law with her, figuring I had the right since I was her fiancé. And if that makes me a possessive lunatic, then I guess I am."

"Sounds to me like you were just trying to protect her."

"I planned to marry the woman. Do you think I wanted her in a place like that week after week?"

His heated reply caused Lydia to wonder if he wasn't still in love with Denise. She watched as he raked a hand through his hair and stood. He walked to the window and stared out at the dark nighttime sky. Lydia felt like sobbing. Maybe Alec wasn't the one for her. Maybe Gerald was right. Perhaps his jaded past would, indeed, prove to be far too great a contender.

"With men this is impossible; but with God all things are possible"—Jesus' words from Matthew 19 rang in her heart in a divine reply, and Lydia knew He was telling her she *could* handle it. With the Lord's help, she could. . .and she would!

"I guess this is obstacle number three," Alec said in a discouraged voice from his place at the window.

"No, it's not."

He glanced over his shoulder at her, before turning around. "What do you mean, it's not?"

She picked up the report and began tearing it into pieces. "You explained. I believe you. It's over. Done. . .nothing's left." Standing to her feet, she walked to the fireplace and tossed in the slips of paper. "No obstacle." She smiled.

"Are you telling me you're willing to overlook my past?"

"Only if you're willing to overlook mine."

He grinned. "Oh, right. What's the worst thing you ever did?"

"Um, let's see. . .I stole a pack of gum from the grocery store when I was ten. I couldn't even sleep that night because my conscience bothered me so much."

Alec feigned a gasp. "I'm shocked."

He lifted her chin. "It was as much of a sin as anything you ever did."

He just stood there, eyeing her carefully. "Lydia, if you're serious, I don't ever want you to bring up my past again. Not ever. You know things I never told Denise because I felt I wouldn't grow spiritually, that I'd never get past the shame of that sinful life, if I had a wife reminding me of what a loser I used to be."

"I'll never bring it up again," Lydia promised. She tipped her head, considering him. "But. . ."

"But?"

She hesitated. Dare she even ask him the question foremost on her heart? Did she want to hear the answer?

"Do you still love Denise?" she managed at last.

Alec took a moment to consider his reply. "Sort of. . .do you still love Michael?"

It was not the response she'd hoped for. In fact, it was the one she dreaded most. But she answered him in spite of her quivering chin. "That's different. Michael's in heaven. He can't show up one day and take me away from you."

A grin spread across Alec's face. "Denise isn't ever going to take me away from you, either. But I loved her enough to ask her to be my wife, and those feelings don't just disappear in three months."

With a sorrowful, audible sigh, Lydia turned and plopped down on the sofa. "Your past isn't obstacle number three," she stated forlornly. "Denise is."

sixteen

The following morning, Gerald stopped over. He seemed satisfied to find Lydia sufficiently depressed over the situation with Alec, although she didn't divulge last night's events. Then after tousling Tyler's hair and giving Brooke a little hug, he went merrily on his way, causing Lydia to feel even worse. How could he revel in her misery?

Not much later, the doorbell rang and three giggling little girls sprang into the house. It was the day Lydia had promised her daughter she could invite a friend over, and one guest had quickly turned to three.

Outside, it rained off and on while, inside, Lydia conducted a tea party with the girls, set up a board game for them, allowed them to watch a video and finally play with Brooke's dolls. Tyler followed his mother around, grumbling about how stupid girls were, and she quickly decided she wasn't going to please everyone today.

Alec didn't phone, much to her great disappointment. He'd left angry last night—obviously she'd struck a nerve. But Sherry called, and Lydia wound up pouring her heart out while she made supper and waited for the girls' mothers to pick up their children.

"Oh, you poor thing," Sherry cooed sympathetically. She paused, apparently in thought. "Say, why don't y'all come here for a little holiday next weekend? The kids can see each other and we can talk and catch up on everything."

"I'd like that, but. . .I don't know." Lydia wondered how she'd get around her father-in-law. He'd surely discover if she disappeared for a whole weekend, and he wouldn't stand for her visiting with the Smiths.

"Let's ask the Lord to make a way," Sherry suggested.

"How 'bout it?"

"If the Lord makes a way," she agreed on a discouraged note, "then, yes, we'll come."

Soon Brooke's friends' parents arrived and took their little girls home. Lydia served dinner and forced herself not to glance next door.

After supper, she cleaned up and the telephone rang. Drying her hands on a dish towel, she answered it, glad to hear Alec's voice.

"Were you planning on coming to the Bible study?" he asked in a somewhat brusque tone.

"I don't have a sitter," she said, wishing she would have remembered and tried to find someone to stay with Tyler and Brooke.

"I guess that's a no, huh?"

"It's a no."

"Okay, then. See ya."

When Alec hung up, Lydia tried not to feel hurt by his abruptness. No doubt he was smarting, too. Was love really supposed to hurt this much? She reflected on her relationship with Michael. They'd had their lovers' quarrels, but at least she'd always felt secure about her future with him.

For the rest of the evening she fell into her usual Saturday night routine, supervising her children's baths, tucking them in, and preparing her lesson for Sunday morning. Oddly, the subject was joy.

Great, she thought on a cynical note. *I'll be a first-rate hypocrite teaching this topic in the mood I'm in.* After further speculation, the Lord changed her heart. She realized her happiness couldn't be dependent on another individual. People weren't perfect. They'd always disappoint her, and they'd always let her down. But God never would. And even though she'd known that fact all along, she'd never put it into practice. She built her whole world around Michael and, after the kids were born, she'd made her family the very reason for her being. When he died, she transferred her dependence to

Gerald—and now, having met Alec, she was slowly beginning to rely on him to supply her joy. But that wasn't right, either.

Heavenly Father, forgive me, she silently pleaded. *My joy needs to come from You.*

She stayed in prayer a few more minutes and then, turning her attention back to her lesson, she felt much more prepared to teach her class.

≫

"Now, while I'm away," Gerald was saying the following afternoon as they dined together at Lydia's house, "I've instructed Sim to check on you."

"I don't need checking," Lydia insisted, more than a touch miffed as she refilled her father-in-law's coffee cup. "I'll be fine."

"But I'm going to be gone at least two weeks, and—"

"Gerald, I can manage on my own. If anything comes up, I'll phone you in Florida."

He didn't reply, but thanked her as he reached for his cup. "In addition to making sure my wife is in good spirits, I hope to convince Mary and her husband to move back to Woodruff," he stated, changing the subject which, to Lydia, meant he had no intention of heeding her request.

Setting down the coffeepot, she almost groaned aloud, thinking of having to deal with Sim Crenshaw for the next couple of weeks. But at least she'd be free to see Sherry!

"I'm convinced my dear daughter and her husband are attending a weak church," Gerald continued. "Sounds lukewarm, and Mary has adopted some very liberal ideas."

"Like what?" Tyler wanted to know, sitting across from Lydia with Brooke on his right side.

"Young man," Gerald reprimanded, "this is an adult conversation. Children should be seen and not heard. Is that clear?"

"Yes, sir." The boy glanced at his mother before looking down at his plate.

"This is what I mean, Lydia. Tyler needs a father."

"Mr. Alec would make a good one," Tyler piped in. But at

Gerald's menacing gaze, he immediately quieted and resumed eating.

Her father-in-law never prohibited her children from voicing their opinions or asking questions before. *He must be under a tremendous amount of pressure*, Lydia thought. Nevertheless, she wasn't going to allow him to coerce her into an unwanted relationship with Sim or any other man.

"Gerald," she began, "I'm praying about it—about a father for my children, a husband for me, except I'd like God to do the choosing, not you. Please don't be offended," Lydia quickly added. "I'm not trying to sound ungrateful. But the fact is, I do not like Simeon Crenshaw and I want you to stop pushing him on me."

"Grampa?" Brooke asked sweetly.

"What is it, dear?"

"Mama's gonna marry Mr. Alec. Me 'n' Ty already 'cided that."

"That's a fun game, but in real life children can't decide anything. That's why they have a mother and a *father*." With a raised brow, Gerald branded Lydia with a scalding glare before turning his attention back to Brooke. "But your mother can't marry Mr. Alec. He is a bad man."

"Gerald!" Lydia's tone sounded sharp to her own ears.

"Well, it's the truth."

"No, it's not!" Tyler spouted angrily.

"This is getting out of hand," Lydia said, trying to curb the sudden tension. "We're not going to discuss Mr. Alec anymore."

Ignoring her, Gerald continued, "Tyler, Brooke, a trusted friend of mine looked into all the things Mr. Alec has ever done and they are very, very bad."

"Your friend is wrong!" Tyler yelled, pitching his fork. It clanged against his glass of milk, and Brooke gasped. "You're wrong, too, Grampa! Wrong!" He shot up off his chair and ran from the dining room, pounding his feet up the stairs where, at last, he slammed his bedroom door. The echo reverberated through the house.

"That boy needs a firm hand," Gerald muttered through a clenched jaw. "Sim could modify his attitude in a minute."

"Who's Sim?" Brooke wanted to know, looking confused.

"He's someone I went to dinner with when you slept over at Gramma and Grampa's house," Lydia explained. "And you met him. He stopped by one evening—the same day the Smiths moved away. He's got dark hair that's sort of bushy. . ."

"Oh, him," Brooke said, wrinkling her little nose. "He got-salotta perfume on!"

Lydia tried not to chuckle at her daughter's remark, but it was true; Sim wore far too much cologne. The night she'd gone out with him, she'd ended up with a terrible headache. That was the night Alec had come to her rescue.

Glancing at her father-in-law, she realized he found nothing amusing about the turn in conversation. He irritably tossed his napkin onto his plate. "I see you've succeeded in brainwashing my grandchildren." He stood.

Lydia did likewise, shocked by the accusation. "I've done no such thing. I've never said a negative word about Sim in front of Tyler or Brooke."

He took a deep breath and his voice softened. "What's happened to you? You've never been an argumentative woman."

"That was always Michael's department, wasn't it?" she stated as tears gathered in the backs of her eyes. She wished Michael were here to handle Tyler and Gerald, but, of course, he wasn't. Then suddenly a vision of Alec, her knight in shining armor, replaced the memory of her late husband. She had no doubt that he would defend her against Gerald's tyranny, and he'd have managed Ty's outburst as well. But the very idea caused her heart to ache all the more since it seemed she'd lost Alec, too.

My joy is in the Lord Jesus, she reminded herself, closing her eyes. *He'll take care of me.*

"I'm leaving," Gerald announced. "See you tonight at church."

" 'Bye, Grampa," Brooke called.

No reply.

ðø

"He's not a bad man," Tyler grumbled, gazing out his bed-room window at Mr. Alec's house. He folded his arms tightly and clenched his jaw.

Suddenly he saw Mr. Alec's truck roll into the driveway. He watched him climb out, look over toward the back door, and for a minute, Tyler wondered if Mr. Alec was going to come over for a visit. He brightened at the thought, but resumed scowling when his new friend just walked into his house instead.

Then he got an idea. He could go ask Mr. Alec about what Grampa said. Yeah! He'd prove Grampa wrong.

Leaving his room, he heard his mother clearing the dining room table. As quietly as he could, he crept downstairs.

"Eat your peas, Brooke," he heard Mama say.

"Tyler didn't eat his peas," she complained.

"Tyler's going to get a spanking for talking back to Grampa. You want one of those, too?"

"No, ma'am, I'll be eating my peas right up. See? I'm eat-ing 'em."

What a little goodie-goodie, Tyler thought with a frown. He'd better make his getaway quick or else!

He inched his way to the kitchen and watched as his mother set a stack of dishes in the sink. He waited impatiently until she walked back into the dining room. Then, sneaking to the back door, he made his escape. Outside, he stayed close to the house, feeling like a spy in a movie he and Matt watched on TV. When he reached the front, he ran fast across the lawn and up the cement steps to Mr. Alec's front porch. Ringing the bell, he plastered his body flat against the house in case his mother should happen to glance out the window.

The door creaked open.

"Pssst. Mr. Alec. Over here."

Tyler peered around the corner frame of the screen door.

"Tyler, what are you doing? Hiding?"

"Uh-huh. I can't let my mama see me."

"How come?" Frowning, Mr. Alec came out and sat down

on the brick porch rail, blocking the view between his house and Tyler's.

" 'Cause I'm supposed to be getting a lickin' about now."

"Oh, yeah?" Tyler heard the smile in Mr. Alec's voice. "What did you do?"

"Sassed my grampa."

He chuckled. "Well, you can't come over here seeking refuge." Mr. Alec stood and got ready to go back inside.

"No. Wait. I gotta talk to you. That's why I came over."

Slowly, he sat back down. "Okay. What's up, kid?"

Tyler swallowed. "My grampa says you're a bad man, but I don't believe him. I think you're a good man."

Mr. Alec looked a little mad, and Tyler wondered if maybe he shouldn't have told him.

"You know what? I was a bad man," Mr. Alec began. His face seemed much friendlier all of a sudden. "But it was a long time ago. Then I heard about what Jesus did on the cross, and I believe He died for all the rotten things I did. I became a Christian and didn't want to be a bad man anymore—and I'm not. Except I'm not perfect, either."

Tyler nodded. "We're all bad till Jesus saves us."

"Right."

He frowned. "But how come Grampa said that stuff about you?"

Mr. Alec had to think about the question for a while. Finally, he said, "Sometimes we look at how bad a person used to be and forget to see how far Jesus has brought him. Take me, for instance. It seems like your grampa is only looking at all the sin that used to be in my life instead of giving me a chance to show him that God helped me change my ways. But don't be angry at him, kid. He's just trying to protect your mom, you, and Brooke."

"Mama wouldn't care if you sinned before—and I don't, either."

Mr. Alec grinned a little. "Yeah, I know."

"And she can make real good chocolate cake. We were

supposed to have it after lunch, but—"

"Hey, you don't have to sell me on your mother, okay?"

"No, I don't want to sell her." Tyler couldn't believe grown-ups could be so dumb. "I just want you to like her."

Mr. Alec put his head back and laughed. "I do like her. I like her a lot. Now, you get yourself home and take your punishment like a man."

"What's that mean?" Tyler asked slowly, not liking the sound of this.

"A man takes his punishment without complaining, and he doesn't cry."

Tyler sighed. "Good thing I'm not a man, 'cause Mama's spankings hurt real bad." His rear end stung just thinking about it.

"Tyler? Tyler. . ." Mama's voice came from the driveway right behind Mr. Alec.

"Uh-oh. Reckoning time." Mr. Alec grinned as if he thought it was funny.

"Couldn't you just talk to her for a while?" Ty whispered pleadingly. "She'll forget about me if you talk to her."

Mr. Alec scratched his jaw, and Tyler guessed he was thinking about it.

"Pleeeeze?" he begged.

"Tyler. . . ," Mama called once more.

"He's right here, Lydia," Mr. Alec replied over his shoulder. Then he gave Tyler a wink.

Tyler sighed with relief.

Mama came up to the porch slowly. "What are you doing here?" she asked with one of those curiously annoyed expressions Tyler had seen plenty of times before.

"Just talkin', Mama," he said innocently.

He turned to their neighbor for help, but realized Mr. Alec was staring at Mama hard. . .like it hurt or something. Glancing at his mother, he saw she was staring right back. Was she going to cry?

It seemed like a whole hour before Mr. Alec cleared his

throat. "You got any pop over at your house yet, Lydia?"

"What?" Mama seemed confused by the question.

"I thought maybe I could come over and we could talk. Actually, I wanted to share something that happened at the Bible study last night. Oh, by the way, the gang says, 'hi.' "

A little smile tugged at the corners of Mama's mouth. "Yes, I'd like to hear all about it. But you'll have to bring your own soft drink. I didn't get to the grocery store yesterday."

"Okay." Mr. Alec stood and walked toward the door.

"And give me a few minutes, would you, Alec?" Mama asked sweetly. "My son and I have unfinished business."

Rats! She didn't forget!

Mr. Alec gave Tyler a slug in the arm—the kind friends gave each other. "Sorry, kid, I tried."

"Thanks," Tyler answered glumly as he trudged home behind his mother.

seventeen

Lydia wound her way through the Monday morning rush-hour traffic heading for Charlotte as she drove Gerald to the airport. Even more nerve-wracking than the bumper-to-bumper traffic jams was having to listen to him giving her instructions.

"Make sure the office supply company delivers the four new chairs for the meeting room."

"I will."

"And help Pastor Camden get the flyers created for our Easter program. It'll be here before we know it."

Lydia promised to do her best and then pulled alongside the curb at the terminal.

"Lastly, I want you to let Sim know your whereabouts at all times, what with that madman living next door to you. There's no telling when he might strike."

"Alec is not a madman," Lydia said, desperately trying to keep her temper in check. "Please don't call him that. I'm in love with him."

"Spare me. I don't have time for this now!"

Lydia clamped her mouth shut. How could she have been so wrong about Gerald? He didn't care about her. How could he? He refused to lend a sympathetic ear.

"Stay away from him," her father-in-law warned. He narrowed his dark gaze for emphasis.

Tightening her grip on the minivan's steering wheel, Lydia gazed out the windshield and took a deep, calming breath. "I don't want to stay away from him," she confessed. "I love him and he loves me. Granted, we have a few things to work out, but—"

"Listen to me!" Gerald shouted, grabbing her arm roughly. Lydia gasped in surprise and pain. Suddenly, as if realizing what he'd done, her father-in-law released her. "Forgive me, dear. I have so much on my mind right now. The district attorney is threatening me with all kinds of nasty business—all of it unwarranted, of course. I can't imagine how Sim convinced him to let me leave the state for the next ten days." He gave her an indulgent smile. "In any event, I can't handle any more problems. For your own good, take my advice.

Lydia didn't answer. On one hand, she felt sorry for him and on the other, she was determined not to allow him to rule her life any longer. But for now, she didn't argue further, fearing Gerald would change his mind and stay home. She had made wonderful plans with Sherry for the upcoming weekend and, having been invited, Alec agreed to go along. They'd had such a special time together yesterday afternoon, sharing things from the Bible and describing how God used His Word to shape their lives. If Lydia ever questioned Alec's faith, she didn't anymore. He loved the Lord with all his heart.

Now if only Gerald would see it.

"Be a good girl while I'm gone," he told her in a voice he would have just as easily used with Brooke.

"Of course," she replied tartly. "I'm always a good girl."

After considering her for a long while, he hopped out of the van, and he hailed a porter to carry his luggage. "I mean it, Lydia," he said finally, "don't cross me." With that, he slammed the door with more force than necessary.

She winced before pulling away from the curb, aware that she was destined for trouble. She fully intended to "cross" her father-in-law, and the consequences frightened her. Not only would she not have Gerald's financial support, Lydia surmised she'd be church disciplined for her disobedience. Just like her mother.

Mama. Lydia now had much more compassion for her mother's situation. And as she drove through Charlotte, she suddenly longed to see her. Lydia needed to ask her forgiveness—how could she have been so blind? Worse, she hadn't even tried to get to know her stepfather. Lydia had a feeling he was probably a very nice man.

Heeding her heart's desire, she stopped at a gas station and phoned for directions.

"Oh, honey, I'm so glad you're coming by." Her mother's voice rang with happiness.

"I'll be there shortly." Hanging up the receiver of the pay phone, Lydia climbed back behind the wheel of the minivan and headed for her mother's new house.

&

By Thursday, Alec felt dead-dog tired. He'd put in forty-two hours the last three days. What was Greg Nivens's problem, anyway? The guy was moody and short-tempered lately. Couldn't be their latest project. Everything was running smoothly.

"Hey, Corbett, I need to talk to you!"

As Alec pulled out his cup of coffee from the machine in the back of the shop, he turned, hearing Greg's voice. "Yeah, what's up?"

"C'mon into my office."

Grudgingly, Alec complied.

"Have a seat," Greg said.

Alec lowered himself into one of the cracked leather chairs in front of his supervisor's paper-strewn desk.

"I've got a message for you."

"And what's that?"

"Stay away from Lydia Boswick."

Alec couldn't conceal his surprise. "Lydia? What's she got to do with anything?"

"You've been over at her house every night this week."

"So. It's none of your business." Alec tipped his head. "And how'd you know I've been at her house?"

His face flushed crimson. "I just do."

"What, are you tailing me? Get a life!" Alec stood and headed for the door.

"Come back here. We're not done yet."

"Yes, we are. You want to discuss business? Fine. But my personal life is just that. Personal."

"This is about your job, Corbett."

Alec halted in his tracks. Turning slowly, he scrutinized the other man. Greg just stood there, rubbing his chin and looking tense. "I think your involvement with Mrs. Boswick," he stated woodenly, "is affecting the quality of your work."

"Oh, yeah?" Alec stepped back into the office and suddenly Larry's words from last week reverberated in his head. *Pastor Boswick has a lot of clout around here. Knows people in high places. If he doesn't like you, he'll make your life miserable.* "You're a member of SPCC, aren't you? So the message you just gave me is from Gerald Boswick. . .? How much did he pay you to harass me?" He shook his head disbelievingly. "Man, I thought you were a Christian."

"This has nothing to do with me," Greg replied as he shifted uncomfortably. "Your work is. . .is suffering."

"Right," he said sarcastically. "So much so that you gave me a bonus last week."

"Corbett, I'm warning you. I'll have to write you up if this keeps going."

"Do what you have to. But I'll see Lydia when and where I please. It's a free country—at least it was the last time I heard. But you did your part, Nivens, so you ought to get your blood money. Except, I've got to tell you," Alec added with a deliberate smirk, "don't quit your day job. You're a terrible actor."

Exiting the office, Alec tossed his coffee into the nearest trash bin. He'd never felt so angry in his life. He had thought Greg was a friend—a brother in Christ. And the disappointment suddenly filling his being overshadowed his fury. *But, Lord, You're bigger than Greg Nivens and Gerald Boswick, and I'm thankful I've got You on my side!*

❧

"Oh, Alec, I'm so sorry," Lydia said that night as they stood in their respective backyards, talking over the fence. She'd just arrived home after being at church for Thursday evening worship service. "Even more than sorry," she added, "I'm embarrassed. I can't believe my father-in-law would go to such lengths to keep us apart. Threatening you with your job?" She shook her head. "I'm shocked."

"I'm not. I hate to tell you, honey, but this seems to be typical behavior for your father-in-law."

She winced, hearing the cynicism in Alec's voice, and yet she could hardly blame him. "Do you want to call it quits?" she asked, her throat tightening with emotion. "I'd understand."

"Would you?"

She shrugged, lowering her gaze. She kicked at a clump of dirt near a fence post. Who was she trying to fool? She'd be heartbroken if they broke up.

"No, I don't want to call it quits," he said at last, causing her to sigh inwardly with relief. "I'm no wimp. Your father-in-law doesn't scare me, but he sure makes me angry." Alec put a booted foot on the fence and leaned forward. "The way I see it is we're battling a social issue. If I rubbed elbows with the elite, wore the right clothes, attended the right church, and wasn't a 'Yankee,' everything would be just fine." He paused, his voice softening. "Do you want to call it quits?"

"No." Lydia nibbled her lower lip in consternation, then glanced at her house. Tyler and Brooke had gone in ahead of her. "Alec, I need to get my children into bed."

"Go ahead. I'll call you in about an hour and we can talk some more, okay?"

Within the hour, Lydia had managed to tuck her two children into bed. They weren't sleeping when Alec phoned, but she had a feeling they were well on their way. They'd never gotten home after school because Lydia had been so busy with office work, so they'd stayed right through until the evening service. Such days made for exhausted children by nine-thirty at night.

"So how was your day?" Alec asked.

"Long," she replied, changing into her nightgown while holding the cordless phone between her ear and shoulder.

"Hey, don't complain to me about long days. I've already put over fifty hours in this week."

"Yes, but you're a man," Lydia said teasingly. "You're

made to handle such hardships."

Alec groaned. "Excuse me, Miss Southern Belladonna. How could I have forgotten such a thing?"

She laughed softly, wondering if Alec really saw her as a belladonna. She had a feeling he wasn't accustomed to women behaving like women, but rather he was used to them being loud and tough—even competing with men.

"Will you tell me what Denise was like?" she blurted without really thinking it through. "I mean, I just want to know what kind of woman she was, how she won your heart."

There was silence for a long spell and Lydia was about to apologize for getting so personal. But then Alec spoke up.

"Denise was fun. She liked to go to basketball games, and. . . well, you remember Debbie from the Bible study, right?"

"Of course."

"Denise was a lot like her."

"I didn't think you liked Debbie. You two acted more like enemies than friends."

Alec chuckled. "Yeah, some people said that about me and Denise, too."

"Well, I hope you won't mind my saying so, but that doesn't seem quite right."

"Guess it wasn't quite right in God's eyes, either, because look what happened."

"Hmm. . ." Clad in her nightgown, Lydia felt chilled and crawled into bed where she could finish her conversation with Alec in cozy comfort.

Then suddenly she heard the front door close downstairs. *Odd*, she thought, *Tyler and Brooke are up here in bed.*

Thinking it might be the wind that rattled this old house frequently, she relaxed, but then decided she'd better check on the children just in case Tyler had come up with one of his bright ideas. Flipping back the covers, she swung her legs off the bed and padded as far as the doorway when she heard the scuff of a hard-sole shoe against the floor at the bottom of the stairs.

"Hey, Lydia. You're so quiet. Did I say something to offend you?"

"No, but. . ." She retreated a few steps. "Alec," she whispered into the phone, "someone's in my house." Panic ripped through her as she wondered how she'd protect her precious children from an intruder.

"You sure?"

The stairs creaked in protest under the weight of her uninvited guest's footfalls. "Yes, I'm sure."

"Hang up and call the cops. I'm on my way over."

With shaky hands, Lydia did as Alec instructed, simultaneously pulling on her robe. She crept into Brooke's room, the closest of the three, and hid behind the door, whispering her address to the 911 operator.

"Please hurry," she murmured fearfully.

"A squad is on the way, ma'am."

In the darkened hallway, Lydia saw the shadowy figure walk across the landing before climbing the last four stairs.

"Mama?"

"Shh. . . ," she silenced her daughter, but only too late. The intruder had heard. He turned toward the sound of Brooke's voice and the soft light from Lydia's bedroom illuminated his features. "Sim!" she gasped, feeling both alarmed and indignant, "what are you doing here?"

He stepped closer, and she wrapped her robe more tightly around her as if it were some kind of shield. "I just came to check on you," he said in an eerie-sounding tone.

"Ch-check on me?" she stammered. "You nearly gave me heart failure. How did you get into my house?"

He dangled a single gold key just above her head. As she looked up at it, he brought his mouth down in a vampirelike swoop and kissed her neck. Lydia shrieked in shock and disgust and, pushing him away, she brought her palm hard against his cheek in a sound slap.

"You'll pay for that," he promised maliciously.

"Mama!" Brooke screamed from her bed.

"It's all right. Don't be afraid," Lydia tried to assure her daughter as her own heart hammered wildly.

Lydia could hear Alec pounding furiously on the door as Sim grabbed her, pulling her toward her bedroom. Brooke began to wail. The phone clunked to the floor as Lydia fought her aggressor with all her might. Tyler emerged from his room just then.

"Mama!"

Before she could utter a word, Sim's rough hand clamped over her mouth. But thankfully Ty drew his own conclusions and ran down the steps. It seemed to take forever before Lydia heard Alec coming. By then, Sim, crazed with evil intent, had her cornered.

"Don't do this, Sim. Stop!"

In a flash he was yanked away, and Lydia watched in a mixture of horror and relief as Alec's powerful fists delivered several well-directed blows. Sim suddenly resembled a life-size rag doll being pushed and pummeled across the room.

"No, Alec," she cried, "don't kill him!"

Sim's body collided with her mirrored bureau, sending pictures, her jewelry box, and perfume bottles crashing to the floor. At last he lay in a heap near her closet.

"Mama! Mr. Alec! The police are here! I let 'em in!" Tyler shouted above the din of Brooke's hysteria.

As the two officers entered the room, Alec breathlessly explained what had happened, and Lydia gathered Brooke into her arms, trying to soothe her. It was then Lydia realized she'd been sobbing, too.

eighteen

Brooke lay fast asleep on Lydia's lap in a rocking chair in the far corner of the living room. Thankfully, Lydia had been able to dress before giving her statement to police. Then Sim was transported to the hospital, where he regained consciousness and appeared fine for the most part. The authorities said he'd be arraigned later. Unfortunately, the sirens brought folks from their homes all up and down the street, and Lydia felt so ashamed and embarrassed. She was only too grateful for Alec, who stepped in and answered questions.

"What a lousy way to meet the neighbors," he remarked facetiously after he saw the last of them out the door. The police had just left as well. Walking through the hallway to the living room, he paused beneath the threshold and gave Lydia a troubled stare. "You sure you're okay?"

Hearing the note of concern in his voice, she felt like sobbing all over again, but managed a weak nod.

Alec strode toward her and, reaching the chair, he hunkered beside it. "First thing in the morning, I want you to call a locksmith and get him to come and change the locks."

"I thought about it," Lydia replied. "But Ron Zimmerman is the only locksmith in Woodruff and since he's a member of SPCC, I'm afraid he'll give my father-in-law a key."

Alec looked momentarily thoughtful. "Well, I could do it, but I have to work a half day, so I won't get to it till the afternoon. Is that all right?"

"Fine. I'm taking the day off tomorrow anyway. I have every intention of phoning Gerald in Florida and reporting this awful incident." Lydia sniffed back a fresh onslaught of tears.

"I just hope he's not the one behind it."

"Oh, Alec, I wondered the same thing." Lydia shook her

head ruefully. "But it's incomprehensible—my own father-in-law, a man whom I have trusted completely for almost three years, the person I counted on to care for and protect the children and me. . . . How could he be even remotely involved with tonight's episode? And yet, with everything that's happened lately, I can't help but think it's possible."

Alec stood to his feet and ran a hand through his blond hair. "Even so, it's doubtful we'll ever prove it." He pursed his lips, inclining his head slightly. "Okay, what about this weekend? Still want to go visit your friends?"

"Most definitely. I need to get away for a while."

"Good. I was hoping you'd say that."

Lydia suddenly glanced around the side of him. "Where's Tyler?"

"Oh. . ." Alec chuckled and motioned toward the front door with his thumb. "He walked out with one of the officers to see the inside of a police car. I didn't think it'd hurt anything. In fact, I thought it might even get his mind off what happened tonight."

As if on cue, the door opened and slammed shut—Tyler style. "That was awesome!" he declared, bouncing into the living room. "Mr. Alec, you shudda seen the stuff they all got in there. Radios, and—"

Alec put a finger to his lips to shush him, but too late.

"Mama," Brooke whimpered.

Lydia frowned at her son for being so noisy. On the other hand, she felt relieved that he wasn't traumatized like Brooke.

Rousing the sleepy girl on her lap, Lydia sat forward. "Y'all had better get to bed. It's very late."

The little girl suddenly began crying again. "No, Mama, I don't want to go to bed. That bad man will come back."

"No, he won't," Lydia said soothingly. "Shh. . ." She stroked her silky blond hair comfortingly.

"He can't come back, Brooke," Tyler told her, "the police got him."

"That's right," Alec added, lowering himself to her eye

level. "He won't hurt you or your mom anymore. It's okay to go to bed now."

"I don't wanna!" With that she buried her face in Lydia's sweater.

"She's overtired," Lydia softly explained. "She can sleep in my bed tonight."

Alec straightened his tall frame. "All right. Guess I'll let you do your mother-thing and I'll get myself home."

Nodding, Lydia got up from the rocker, holding Brooke in her arms. "I can't thank you enough for your help tonight. I don't know what I would have done if you hadn't—"

"Don't even think about the what ifs. It's over. Try to forget it, all right?" Alec turned. "G'night, kid," he said to Tyler. He gave him a sort of sideways hug with one arm slung around his shoulders. "Help your mom out, and I'll see you tomorrow."

"Sure."

"Come and lock the door after me."

"Okay. . .I know how to lock it real tight."

"I know you do."

With a little smile, Lydia bid Alec good night and climbed the stairs. She felt Brooke's small arms encircle her neck in a death grip as the little girl began to cry, and Lydia tried not to hate Simeon Crenshaw for terrorizing her family—and her!

❧

On Friday, Alec expertly changed Lydia's locks, and then, under a clear, sunny sky, Lydia and Alec packed up her mini-van and drove off toward Tennessee. On Interstate 40, the mountains rose up like smoke, for which they were named, and spanned the horizon like charcoal sashes against an azure sky. The highway dipped and peaked, between towering rock formations, then it stretched across wide forested valleys.

Tyler chatted incessantly for the first part of the journey. He asked Alec, who sat behind the wheel, every kind of question his eight-year-old mind could imagine. Did he like dogs? "Yep." How about cats? "Hate 'em."

The conversation continued for a while longer, and then Ty

grew bored and sat back to play one of his hand-held electronic games while Brooke watched on curiously. They still had four and a half hours before reaching Nashville.

"Brooke seems to be calmer today," Alec remarked to Lydia in a hushed tone so Brooke wouldn't overhear.

"Yes. In the daylight, everything that happened last night seems like a nightmare instead of real life. I just hope she'll be able to forget it easily enough."

Alec nodded reflectively. "Know what I realized last night?"

"What?"

"I realized how much I've really come to care about you and the kids. I wanted to kill that guy—not a very Christian-like response, is it?"

"Oh, I don't know. You were protecting us, and Sim wasn't exactly in the right state of mind for a discussion."

"I'll say." Alec momentarily took his eyes off the road and glanced her way. "Know what I also realized?"

"Hmm?"

"I don't love Denise—maybe I never did. It's weird, but I can't ever recall feeling the way I did when I saw Sim with his hands on you. I felt scared and angry all at once. Oh, I've been jealous before. Denise was good at making me feel jealous. But this was different. Much different. And I guess I can't explain it any better than I just tried."

Lydia looked down at her hands, folded neatly in her lap, and smiled. She couldn't care less that Alec wasn't eloquent when it came to sharing his feelings. He was honest and that was what mattered most to her. Besides, he'd just said the very words she longed to hear. He didn't love Denise!

"Alec, if it took something like last night to cause you to realize your true feelings, then I'll count it no small blessing." Her smile broadened. "You know what I've decided? I've decided God sent you here to rescue me. You're my knight in shining armor."

"Right." He laughed, obviously to cover his sudden embarrassment. "Oh, and speaking of rescuing. . .you never did tell me what your father-in-law had to say this morning."

"He didn't say much—I did most of the talking. I told him how disappointed I felt with him for threatening you and causing you to lose your job. He claimed he didn't know what I was talking about. Then I informed him about what happened last night with Sim, and he got very quiet. Perhaps he felt angry or maybe he felt guilty. I don't know. I couldn't bring myself to ask."

Alec changed lanes, passing a long truck carrying a large piece of machinery. Tyler and Brooke began to chatter excitedly over it.

"Lydia, I'm wondering. . .would you tell me what kind of relationship your husband had with his father?"

"Sure. They were a lot alike in many ways and keep in mind that Michael was an attorney so he loved a good debate." Lydia couldn't help a smile. "He and Gerald had plenty of them."

"About anything specific?"

"Not that I can recall. I know Michael didn't approve of his father involving himself so heavily with the church's finances as well as those of some of the congregation—like my mother, for instance. But I remember Gerald claiming to be a sharp accountant, and he argued that he had a personal interest in the financial success of SPCC and its members." She sighed regretfully. "But Michael would never tell me details. He said he didn't want me worrying over anything. Of course, Elberta never allowed either of us to sit in on the men's conversation and, frankly, I didn't care to. But now I wished I would have paid more attention and asked more questions."

"Your father-in-law drives an awful fancy car—not that I begrudge pastors any luxuries. It's just that when I saw him pulling into your driveway last weekend, it made me all the more suspicious, considering the allegations against him."

"Yes, I know. . . ." Lydia mentally pictured the grand house in which her in-laws resided. She had always thought they'd deserved the "blessing" for being such servants of God, but now she, too, felt suspicious—and it troubled her deeply.

It was almost nine o'clock when Alec found his way to the Smiths' new house west of Nashville. It was located in an elevated subdivision and they drove up a long, winding road whose elevation caused their ears to pop. After they'd parked, Sherry was the first to greet them. Tall and shapely, she had curly honey blond hair that hung slightly past her shoulders.

"Lydia, you sweet thing!" she cried, with outstretched arms.

They embraced before Sherry pulled back, and Lydia found herself looking up into her dear friend's freckled face.

"I'm so sorry, Lyd, will you ever forgive me for shunning you? I swear I hurt myself more than I hurt you."

Tears gathered in Lydia's eyes. "I already forgave you." She sniffed.

Sherry's gaze grew misty as well. "I'm so glad to see you."

"I'm so glad to see you, too."

They embraced again as Jordan Smith walked out of the house. "With these two blubbering over each other," he said to Alec, "I guess we're on our own." He stuck out his right hand and introduced himself just before his three children bounded out the door. All at once there were five little ones squealing happily in the driveway.

"C'mon, Ty, I'll show you my room," Matt said. He was dark-headed like his father and beneath the yard light, Lydia smiled at the excitement in his brown eyes. "Tomorrow, I'll show you the tree house Daddy built. No girls allowed."

"Cool!" Tyler replied.

The boys took off in a flash with the girls laughingly chasing after them.

"Why don't y'all come on inside?" Jordan invited. "And, Alec, let me help you with the luggage."

With her arm around Lydia's shoulders, Sherry ushered her into the living room.

"So what do you think about Alec?" Lydia whispered. "I want your first impression."

"He's quite tall."

Lydia tossed a maroon throw pillow at her friend. "You're so observant."

Sherry laughed and tossed it back.

"And here they are," Jordan said facetiously, "taking out the living room already." He shook his dark head and walked in with Alec right behind him. "You two are worse than the kids."

Lydia glanced at Alec, who sent her an affectionate wink before lowering himself into a mauve swivel rocker. Lydia remembered when the Smiths bought this living room ensemble, couch and two chairs, glass-top coffee table and matching end tables. And she recalled vividly just how excited Sherry had been the day it arrived. It was just before Michael died.

She gazed at Sherry, then Jordan, and back to Sherry once more. "You two are a sight for sore eyes, do you know that?" Her throat constricted with unshed emotion.

"So are you."

"Oh, will you two knock it off," Jordan muttered irritably.

"I see he hasn't changed a bit," Lydia told Sherry.

Sherry, in turn, looked at Alec. "My husband has no patience for female sensibilities," she explained. "But I hope you do. Lydia and I can cry at the drop of a hat, can't we, honey?"

Jordan's expression was oblique as he faced Alec. "Do y'all play Ping-Pong? I've got a table set up in the rec room. How 'bout a game?"

"You're on." Alec seemed relieved. Standing, he crossed the room, trailing Jordan.

"Oh, Sherry, you scared him off," Lydia said in mild rebuff. "We've only known each other a month."

"If he scares that easily," she drawled in reply, "then he ain't a man worth having. Besides, if Tyler hasn't spooked him by now, chances are he's a keeper."

They laughed together.

"You've changed," Sherry said at last.

"I have?"

"Uh-huh. You look. . .happy again."

"I feel happy again," Lydia admitted.

"I'm so glad. Come on," she said, holding out her hand. "I'll show y'all around the rest of the house. I just love it here!"

Lydia stood and as she toured her good friend's nicely decorated home, she recognized objects that had once hung on the walls of a different house, in a different state. So familiar and yet strange in their new environment that they might as well have been brand new, and suddenly Lydia was reminded of herself. Things around her had changed dramatically. She looked the same on the outside, but she could hardly claim to be the person she'd been a month ago. She was finally back among the living.

And it was all because the Lord had brought Alec Corbett into her life.

nineteen

"You're awfully quiet," Alec remarked during the drive homeward late Sunday night.

"Just thinking."

"Did you have a nice weekend?"

Lydia smiled. "Very nice." From the passenger seat, she glanced over her shoulder into the back, where Tyler and Brooke slept peacefully. "How about you? Did you enjoy meeting the Smiths?"

"Yeah. Nice people."

"And you really didn't mind bunking down in the family room with two rambunctious boys?" Lydia couldn't suppress a giggle. "Did you get any sleep at all?"

"Some." The lights from the highway illuminated his rugged features and Lydia saw the smirk on his face. "Tyler and Matt sure like to talk."

"You've been a good sport, Alec. And you're very patient with children."

"Kids never bothered me. But it seemed Jordan got a little hot under the collar a few times."

"Yes, he has a habit of raising his voice when the children play too loudly. It used to really upset Tyler, but I think in time he grew accustomed to it."

"I remember the first day I met your kids. They asked if I was going to holler at them for standing on the fence." Alec chuckled. "Must have been what Jordan used to do."

"It was."

Alec laughed again. "But the highlight of the weekend was hearing all about you from Sherry."

"I already told you, she exaggerates," Lydia stated with a bit of a huff. She'd like to get even with her longtime friend

149

for sharing those silly stories—like the time they were both expecting babies and Lydia locked herself out of the house after grocery shopping. Sherry came up with the brilliant notion to climb through the window, but in their conditions neither fit. Nevertheless, Sherry had to try and managed to get herself good and stuck. That was when the Woodruff police were called. . .

"The tales I heard," Alec said amusedly, "sounded more like *I Love Lucy* reruns."

"Oh, hush," Lydia replied in mild rebuff, but she laughed softly in spite of herself.

She thought this weekend had been a wonderful blessing. She and Alec had gotten to know more about each other. And he had been a perfect gentleman the whole time—even Sherry commented on it. Somehow her friend's approval affirmed in her heart that God truly had His hand on her relationship with Alec.

"Did the dinner conversation tonight upset you?" he asked, drawing her from her reverie.

Lydia thought it over. The topic had been her father-in-law. "Yes, it upset me," she admitted. "I feel betrayed."

"So you believe the Smiths and your mother?"

Lydia nodded as a vision of her father-in-law handling her roughly in the minivan last Monday flittered through her mind. "I'm convinced Gerald enjoys controlling others, and for so long, I was content to be controlled by him."

"Hmm. . ."

"I am scared though, Alec. When I stand up to him, my father-in-law could very well pull the rug of security right out from under me."

"I warned you that could happen."

"Yes, you did. . .but I'm not turning back. I can't! I believe the Lord has opened my eyes and allowed me to learn the things I have for a reason. He now expects me to act upon my knowledge even if it means I have to find another job. . . another church."

"I hope you're planning to contact your husband's attorney and find out the specifics regarding any money Michael left you. I'd hate to see what happened to your mother happen to you, too."

"Oh yes, that's another area of my life I intend to take back from Gerald."

Alec chuckled. "You know, for a sweet little Southern thing, you sure are brave. I admire you for that, especially since I've got a feeling many men cower around your father-in-law."

"I'm not so brave. My insides feel like jelly right now." Glancing over at him, Lydia saw the smile on his rugged features broaden. "But, you know, Alec, I think Jordan was right—about us worshiping together."

"I was going to bring up the subject myself." He momentarily took his eyes off the road and looked over at her. "What do you suggest?"

"From what I recall, I liked Pastor Spencer. I wouldn't mind giving his church a try. Of course, Gerald believes Berean Baptist is inferior to SPCC. But I think that might have been an issue Michael would have gone toe-to-toe with his father on."

"Mark's a strong preacher and I think you'll be blessed, but ours is a small church. We're lucky if fifty people show up on Sunday morning. That'll be different for you."

"Yes. SPCC runs about two thousand attendees on any given Sunday morning."

Alec was silent for several miles. At last, Lydia heard him expel a long breath before he spoke again. "You sure about this, Lydia? You sure about me. . .us?"

She smiled, sensing his insecurity. "Don't worry. I won't change my mind no matter what." She paused in earnest. "I just hope you don't."

"Not me."

They continued to chat amicably the rest of the way into Woodruff. Then, as Alec was about to make the turn into Lydia's driveway, she caught sight of Gerald's BMW parked out front.

"Oh no," she murmured. "I thought he was in Florida!"

"Your father-in-law?"

"Yes. But it's nearly midnight. What's he doing here at this hour?"

Gerald's stern countenance suddenly flashed before the headlights as he stepped down from the front porch.

"Judgment day," Alec remarked, bringing the van to a halt near the garage.

"Please don't make jokes. I feel like I might be sick."

"Listen," he stated earnestly, "neither of us has done anything wrong."

Her heart hammering anxiously in her chest, Lydia didn't trust herself to reply. But Gerald would discover their plans eventually; it may as well be now.

Sending up a tiny prayer, she opened the door, climbed out, then pulled on the back door, rousing Tyler and Brooke.

Gerald happened upon her fast. "Where have you been?" Beneath the yard light, Lydia could barely make out his features, although she heard the controlled anger in his voice. "And why doesn't my key work in the lock?"

"Which question would you like me to answer first?" Lydia countered firmly, but politely.

Alec came around, popped the hatch, and began removing luggage from the minivan. Seeing him, Gerald's jaw dropped slightly.

"What in the world have you done? Taking off with a strange man for the weekend? And in front of the children. . ."

"It was all very proper, I assure you," Lydia stated, feeling insulted. She lifted Brooke out of the vehicle, then moved aside so Tyler could jump down.

"Hi, Grampa. Guess what? I got to see Matt this weekend. His dad made him a tree house and it's pretty cool, but Mr. Alec had to finish off the side of it 'cause Mr. Smith isn't as good at building stuff as Mr. Alec."

"Well, well, isn't that. . .nice," came Gerald's barbed reply while he pierced Lydia with his dark gaze. "The Smiths.

You visited the Smiths."

Alec closed the hatch and then tossed Tyler the house keys. "Go open the back door, will you?"

"Sure. I caught those keys good, didn't I?"

"Yep."

Lydia set Brooke down, instructing her to follow her brother into the house.

"But it's dark in there," she whined.

"Ty will turn on the lights," Lydia promised, hating the way Brooke was suddenly so afraid of the nighttime. For the past two nights, Lydia had had to sleep with Brooke so she wouldn't cry.

Once the children were out of earshot, Lydia turned to her father-in-law. "Sherry's my friend and I've missed her."

"I see."

"And just so you know, I visited my mother last Monday."

"Mm. . ."

"Furthermore, Alec and I are still seeing each other."

"So I gathered." He stuck his hands in the pockets of his beige London Fog trench coat. "You've thwarted my every word of warning."

Lydia could only nod.

Gerald grunted. "You certainly know how to hurt an old man. I only wanted the best for you—for my grandchildren—and to have my efforts tossed back in my face is quite distressing."

Experiencing a sudden wave of shame, Lydia chanced a look at Alec and saw him smirk. She wondered what he found amusing. Then leaning casually against the minivan, he met her gaze and mouthed, "Guilt trip."

She nodded back knowingly before facing Gerald again.

Just then Tyler burst out the back door. "Mama, Brooke is screaming her head off and I turned on the lights upstairs. But it didn't help."

"Want me to go in?" Alec asked.

"Would you mind?"

"Nope."

"Wait a moment," Gerald demanded. He turned to Alec, then returned his gaze to Lydia. "Since when does a stranger see after Brooke's welfare?"

"Alec is hardly a stranger." She gave him the go-ahead to proceed to the house before continuing, "And since Sim terrorized all of us last week, Alec is something of a hero in our eyes—especially Brooke's. She feels safe with him. So do Tyler and I for that matter."

"Now there's an oxymoron for you," he stated sarcastically. "You feel safe with a man who's been convicted of offenses such as disorderly conduct and drunk driving? Where's your head, Lydia? In addition, I think you misunderstood Sim's intentions."

"There was no misunderstanding."

"He only came to see after your well-being."

"He attacked me!" Lydia couldn't believe her father-in-law was taking Sim's side against hers. And, yet, she told herself she shouldn't be surprised.

"Sim never meant to cause you any harm. He merely wanted a kiss. He's crazy about you."

"He's crazy. I'll grant you that much."

"Now, listen," her father-in-law said, gently taking hold of her upper arm, "we will discuss your relationship with your, um, *neighbor* another time. But for now, there's a more urgent matter to address. Let's go in the house, send your friend home, and make some coffee while we talk, shall we?"

"Thank you, but no. Whatever you have to say to me, Gerald, you can say out here. I'm tired and I don't feel much like having coffee." She'd never dared to speak to her father-in-law that way and she felt a bit amazed at herself. Next, she pulled her arm from his grasp.

"Very well." He inhaled deeply, audibly. "I must insist you drop any litigation against Sim. He's not even going to sue your *hero* for assault and battery. Isn't that a relief?"

"He doesn't have a case. Why would he sue Alec?"

"Lydia, two men were fighting in your bedroom—one had the key to your house, the other has a criminal record. This could get very ugly and my point is this—with all the bad publicity out there, we cannot afford anymore. Sim is my attorney. I need him right now. Everything is running smoothly and he expects to have the case against me dismissed by the end of the week. Then Elberta will return and things will fall back into place." He paused, his dark gaze boring down at her. "You wouldn't want to ruin the Boswick family's good name just to get back at Sim, now would you? Vengeance is mine, saith the Lord. I will repay." The threat lingered in the air.

Lydia was tempted to succumb to his persuasion, but soon recognized it as another manipulative ploy. "I'll consider what you've said," she promised, despising the fragility in her own voice. But squaring her shoulders in spite of her trembling emotions, she made her way toward the house.

≈

"I cannot begin to fathom what went through your head last Thursday night!" Gerald glared at Sim's bruised face and swollen eyes. "She hates you. I just left her place and I'm convinced of it. What's more, Lydia seems more determined than ever to continue her little liaison with Alec Corbett."

"So that's what brought you back from Florida so early." Sim's puffy lips twisted into a cynical grin. "And here I thought you were worried about me."

Gerald snorted in disgust. "You've likely ruined everything."

"Not so fast. Not so fast. I've come up with a plan."

"Oh? And what might that be?"

"We'll get rid of that big ox of Lydia's." He rubbed his jaw gingerly and hardened his gaze.

Gerald shook his head. "Murder is out of the question. I do have some scruples left, you know."

"I'm not talking about killing the man. We'll just make his life so miserable that he won't want anything more to do with Lydia or the entire Boswick family. We'll get him to leave town."

"Intimidation won't work on him. He'll keep coming back for more. I know his type. And this whole ordeal has already gotten out of control. Such a shame. I almost had Lydia in the palm of my hand. We removed her nosy mother, but managed to keep her funds—that was a plus. You did a splendid job, altering those financial documents."

"Thank you." Sim took a little bow.

"Next we sent those meddlesome Smiths packing. Lydia trusted me. Believed in me. I know I could have convinced her to marry you." He swung a look of contempt Sim's way. "But you blew it. And when Lydia finds out about her trust account, she'll never speak to me again and I'll be denied the privilege of seeing my grandchildren."

"She's not going to find out. Sit down, Gerry," Sim said loosely. "I've got it all planned. You're still going to be the most acclaimed preacher in the United States—perhaps even the world. When we're through, Billy Graham won't be able to hold a candle to you. Your legacy will last for generations to come."

A satisfied warmth coursed through Gerald's veins as he lowered himself into an armchair. He allowed his gaze to wander around Sim's posh, high-rise apartment near downtown Charlotte. Yes, Gerald preferred riches to rags any day. "I gave my life to Christ, sacrificed in those early years, but what has God ever done for me in return? Nothing. He even took my son! Everything I possess now, I've acquired on my own."

"God helps those who help themselves," Sim said. "And after we pull off this little caper, you'll be rich enough to obtain the power you've longed for—worked for." He smiled, a sinister light flickering in his eyes. "And after two years of watching and waiting, I'll finally have half a million dollars. . . and Lydia."

twenty

Lydia threw open the drapes and peered outside as the Monday morning sunshine flooded her bedroom. "Tyler, Brooke. . .time to wake up," she called, walking into the hallway.

Soon nothing short of mayhem broke loose as Brooke tried to find her favorite dress to wear to school and Tyler searched for his gym shoes. Lydia directed their steps from the kitchen while preparing breakfast, then rushed to get herself ready. At last they were all dressed and on their way.

After depositing her children in their respective classrooms, Lydia entered the church offices. To her relief, Gerald behaved as though nothing were amiss and it was business as usual for most of the day. Around two in the afternoon, Lydia managed to discretely place a call to Michael's one-time partner and attorney. His secretary stated that Brian was out of town, but she penciled Lydia in for an appointment late Friday at four o'clock. With that taken care of, Lydia sat back and continued working until Tyler and Brooke were dismissed from school. But, later, as she pulled into her driveway and spotted Alec's truck next door, she had an inkling something was wrong. Alec never got home early on Monday.

As soon as she could, she phoned him, only to hear him knocking on her back door. With an amused grin, she answered it. "Great minds think alike," she greeted. "I was just trying to get a hold of you."

Alec stepped into the house, a dour expression clouding his face. "I lost my job today," he stated abruptly.

Lydia inhaled sharply. "Oh no. . .I wondered what was up when I saw you were home."

"Greg Nivens wouldn't come out and admit I was getting canned because you and I are still seeing each other," Alec continued as he shut the back door behind him. "He just kept saying the quality in my work hasn't been up to company standards and that's a bald-faced lie. But I have a call in to the company's national headquarters, and I E-mailed my old supervisor. I'm planning to appeal."

Lydia didn't know what to say.

"Did you buy any pop yet?" Alec asked, entering the kitchen.

"I'm afraid not," she replied weakly. "I haven't had a chance to go to the grocery store."

"That's a downer."

She followed him in and watched as he collapsed his large frame into a chair near the table. She felt so incredibly responsible for Alec losing his job that hot tears sprang into her eyes. "Oh, Alec, I'm so sorry."

"Forget it. I really didn't want a soft drink anyhow."

"No, not that. . .your job."

He frowned curiously. "It's not your fault the axe fell today."

"Yes, it is."

Alec shook his head. "No, it isn't. And, like I said, I plan to fight this thing. In the meantime, there are plenty of other jobs around. I'm not worried. Besides, I've been employed with Heritage Craft Furniture for a long time. If I don't find employment right away, I'll get some compensation until a hearing takes place."

Lydia didn't feel assuaged in the least.

"Listen," he said finally, standing and walking toward her, "I'm angry. I'll admit it. But not with you. You mean more to me than a lousy job." He shrugged. "I'll get another one. No big deal."

She swallowed a sob. It certainly was a "big deal" and to think Gerald was the motivation behind it all caused her an enormous amount of grief.

Alec put his hands on her shoulders, regarding her intently. "But whatever you do, don't let your father-in-law know my getting fired has upset you. That's what he wants, except we've got God on our side. What can Gerald or anyone else do to us?"

✥

It was a challenge for Lydia to keep quiet the next couple of days—especially when she sensed that her father-in-law enjoyed goading her.

"How's Alec?" he asked on Wednesday afternoon as he thumbed through the mail that had been deposited on her desk.

"He's fine," she replied, trying to sound nonchalant even though her nerves were utterly jangled.

"You know, Elberta has been talking about doing some remodeling, maybe Alec, would like to give me an estimate—since he is a carpenter. I'm sure he'd appreciate the extra money. After all, carpenters don't exactly make a fortune."

Lydia forced a subtle shrug, while inside she was seething with indignation. "You'd have to ask him," she replied offhandedly.

Hours later she left work, still fuming.

But that evening, she attended Berean Baptist's midweek service with Alec, and Pastor Spencer's message lifted her spirits. Afterward, she chatted for several minutes with Debbie and Judy before Alec reintroduced her to the pastor and his wife. Lydia couldn't recall a nicer exchange, and she decided there was something very quaint, personal, even intimate about worshiping the Lord with a smaller body of believers.

"So what did you think?" Alec asked as they walked through the parking lot.

"I liked Children's Church with Mrs. Spencer," Tyler piped in. "Grampa doesn't have anything like that at SPCC cuz he says us kids should sit still and be quiet in regular church."

"It wasn't quiet in Children's Church tonight," Brooke said, shaking her head. "We played a game, sang songs, learned a Bible verse, and even heard a story."

"It's kind of a neat ministry," Alec explained to Lydia.

"Some students from the local Christian college volunteer their time and help Mrs. Spencer." Placing a hand under her elbow, he assisted her into his truck.

"Mama," Tyler asked once Alec closed the door and began walking around to the other side, "is Grampa gonna be mad that we came here tonight?"

"Probably," Lydia replied carefully. "But, even so, he'd never be angry with either you or Brooke."

A sudden burst of cold March wind blew into the truck as Alec opened the door and slid behind the wheel. "Who wants ice cream?"

Cheers hailed from the backseat while Lydia shook her head in amazement. "It's winter and y'all want ice cream?"

"Ice cream's good any time," Tyler said and his little sister quickly agreed.

"You're outnumbered, Lydia," Alec told her as he started up the truck. "Ice cream it is."

It was nearly ten o'clock when Alec finally headed for home. From the silence filling the backseat, Lydia could tell her children were tired. She glanced at them and found that both sat staring dazedly out the window, watching streetlights go by.

"Want to hear my latest wild idea?"

Turning her attention to Alec, Lydia smiled. "Sure."

He paused, turning a corner. "I think I want to start my own business."

"Wonderful."

"Really think so?"

"Certainly. I think working for yourself is much better than doling out weeks, months, and years to a company that doesn't appreciate you."

"My thoughts exactly. Listen to the name I thought up. Yankee Doodle Dandy's Carpentry."

Lydia burst out laughing. "In Woodruff, North Carolina? I don't think so."

"No?"

"No!"

Alec chuckled. "I was just kidding anyway."

"I'm relieved to hear that."

His smile widened as he turned the truck onto their street until a horrific sight greeted them. Red lights glowed from several fire engines, voices echoed from two-way radios, and adding to the pandemonium were shouts from firemen and neighbors.

"Wow! What's happening?" Tyler asked.

Alec pulled the truck to a halt where a policeman had barricaded the entrance to the street. "Major house fire near the end of the block," he said as Lydia's insides did a nervous flip. Was it her place? Had an appliance been left on and ignited somehow? She strained her vision, trying to see.

Alec seemed to be doing the same thing. "That's my house," he finally said. All at once, he killed the engine, climbed out of the truck, and began jogging toward all the commotion.

"Oh, dear Lord, no. . .please don't let it be true." But even as Lydia sent up the plea, a heavy dread settled over her.

"Mama, is Mr. Alec's house really on fire?"

"I hope not."

"Maybe it's really Mrs. Cavendish's. She's old and smokes a pipe on her back porch all the time. Matt said so. . ."

Slowly, Lydia climbed from the truck. She began shivering, not so much from the cold, but from the realization that Alec's house was indeed on fire!

❧

Alec picked his way through the rubble of what had once been his home, thinking he might have believed last night was a nightmare if, when the first pinks of dawn streaked the eastern sky, he'd awakened. But he hadn't, largely because he'd been up all night. And all day.

Despite a valiant effort by firefighters, his house was a total loss.

Neighbors claimed they heard some sort of blast before

flames could be seen jutting from the windows. Many had feared he perished in the blaze until he showed up. Their concern had touched him despite the tumult in his heart.

"Lydia's house has some damage," Larry remarked, crossing the driveway. "But nothing major. . .hey, is she still at her mother's place? She seemed pretty upset last night."

"She wasn't the only one." Alec darted a gaze at his friend, glad he had thought to call Larry on the cellular phone. Larry had been a great source of encouragement. "But, in answer to your question, yeah, Lydia's still at her mom's. . .as far as I know." He hesitated briefly. "Thanks for dropping her and the kids off last night."

"No problem. She was in no condition to drive—even if she'd been able to access her van back there in the garage."

Alec blew out a long breath, turning his gaze to the burned-out remains of the chimney.

"Are you thinking it's arson?" Larry asked, stepping over the charred wreckage and coming to stand beside him.

"It has to be—and that guy from the insurance company who was here earlier seemed to agree. Of course, no one's going to know for sure until the police do their own investigation. But I have a feeling they'll never find the person who's responsible." He faced Larry again. "You know, if I would have come home right after church, I could very easily be dead now—or worse."

"Man, that's God's hand of protection for you!"

"Sure is." Alec swung around and, again, surveyed the incredible scene before him, praising the Lord for sparing his life. Even so, he'd lost everything he owned, except for some of his tools over in the garage. It had suffered minimal damage, but would hardly provide him adequate shelter. Worse, he didn't even have a change of clothes.

"Listen, Alec, you're welcome to stay at my place for as long as you want."

"Thanks," he muttered, discouragement quickly settling in. "I appreciate the offer and everything else you've done. But I think I'll leave town instead."

"What? Why?"

Pivoting, Alec considered his buddy. "He won. Don't you get it? Pastor Boswick got what he wanted—he destroyed me. I mean, I've got two hundred bucks in the bank, fifty dollars in my wallet, along with some credit cards that are almost maxed out. The only clothes I own are on my back. I've got no job, no house. . .even after the insurance comes through— *if* they come through, considering it could be arson—it's going to take me years to gain back my losses. What can I possibly offer Lydia now?"

Larry chuckled lightly and shrugged. "I have a feeling she'd take you as is."

Alec shook his head. "I'd never ask her to."

"Aw, c'mon, don't give up now. God will work it out. In the meantime, I think you'd better stay at my place. Take a shower, get some sleep. . ." Larry glanced at his watch. "I hate to do this to you, but I've got to get to work. My boss stuck me on second shift for the next two weeks. Here are the keys. I'll see y'all later."

Alec turned the house keys in his palm. "Thanks."

"You bet." Larry gave him a parting salute before walking to the street and climbing into his car.

Exhausted to the bone and utterly spent in spirit, Alec climbed into his truck and drove to Larry's place, where he managed to sleep the afternoon away.

twenty-one

Lydia hadn't seen Alec since the fire Wednesday night and here it was Friday afternoon. She feared the worst—that Gerald had succeeded in dissuading Alec from ever wanting to see her again. Perhaps Alec had decided she wasn't worth the trouble. The fact that she couldn't reach Alec on his cell phone and that he hadn't returned any of her voice mail messages only increased her anxiety. Did he blame her after all?

On a long sigh, she glanced at the white contemporary-styled wall clock above the secretaries' station of Josephson, Hamill, and Bosh Law Offices. Four o'clock exactly.

"Lydia?"

At the sound of a man's deep voice, she stood and smiled a greeting. "Hello, Brian."

"How nice to see you again," he said with a genuine inflection. "Come on back to my office and let's talk."

She followed him down a narrow hallway and couldn't help a glance to the left—where Michael's office had been. A man she'd never seen before sat behind a large oak desk, talking on the phone.

"Have a seat," Brian said as she entered his office. "Make yourself comfortable." He lowered himself into a chair across from hers. "How've you been?"

"Good." Lydia managed to smile in spite of the nastiness incurred by her father-in-law.

"So, what can I do for you?" he asked, raking a hand through his professionally groomed short, brownish-blond hair.

Lydia slowly began to explain. "I guess I was just in too much shock to really hear what you told me at the reading of

Michael's will. I wondered if you'd kindly explain things to me again."

"Sure, but your father-in-law is your agent, and he ought to be able to inform you as well as I can."

She hedged, expelling a weary breath. "There's a bit of a problem between Gerald and me. . .unfortunately."

Brian didn't seem surprised. "Forgive me, Lydia, but I never did trust that man. I often wondered why Michael didn't attend church elsewhere since he obviously had very little faith in his own father's ethical stance. But Michael felt convinced he could make a difference with his dad—and perhaps for a time he did. But from what I've been hearing, Gerald Boswick has finally crossed the line."

Standing, Brian walked to his file cabinet and retrieved a folder. He opened it and scanned the terms of Lydia's trust account before defining them for her one by one. When he was through, she stared back at Brian in mild shock.

Suddenly everything made sense, sickening as it was.

"A one million dollar trust?"

Brian nodded. "Because you haven't been eligible to draw from its principal yet, you've only received quarterly dividend checks, generated by the interest."

"And to be *eligible*, I have to. . .remarry?"

"That's right. Michael feared Southern Pride Community Church would somehow end up absorbing your bequest," Brian stated more cynically than emphatically, "and he took great pains to be sure such a thing wouldn't happen while ensuring that you were well taken care of in the meantime. He wanted there to be a two-year interim, which expired over six months ago, so now if you remarry, the money is yours in full."

That's why Gerald wanted me to marry Sim, Lydia silently concluded. *They're in this together. Neither loves nor cares about me. They just want my money!* Tears pooled in her eyes at the realization. "I feel so betrayed," she murmured. "All this time, I trusted him."

Brian frowned. "Has something happened?"

"Oh yes." Lydia spilled the entire story—about Alec and how she loved him, but how Gerald forbade her to see him, pushing Sim on her instead. She detailed the break-in, Alec losing his job, and finally the fire that destroyed his house. By the time she finished, she was weeping openly, and Brian handed her a box of tissues.

"Lydia," he said solemnly, sitting forward with his elbows braced on his knees, "we've got to call the police. Right now. They need to hear everything you just told me."

He didn't have to convince her. She readily agreed.

ð

By the glow of his large flashlight, Alec loaded his arms with tools from his garage. Since Lydia's house was dark next door, he figured now would be a good time to gather up his stuff and get out of here—before she came home. Alec had no intention of talking to her, much less telling her good-bye. But good-bye it was. He'd had a good forty-eight hours to work himself into an emotional black hole, and he'd concluded that he would make her one unfit spouse. What had he been thinking? He'd lived a veritable fairy tale the past six weeks. But reality had delivered its staggering blow. His future seemed as bleak as his present-day situation, not to mention his sorry past.

Walking to his truck, Alec deposited the tools into the backseat beside his duffle bag containing the new jeans, underwear, and a few sweatshirts he'd managed to purchase. Now, with a full tank of gas, he planned on driving until his pickup ran out of fuel. Wherever he found himself, he'd stay. Maybe he'd find work. So what if he lived the rest of his life alone? He ought to be used to it by now.

"Alec?"

He froze at the sound of Lydia's soft voice coming from behind him. Then he inwardly cursed his misfortune. Why did she have to show up now?

Straightening slowly, he expelled a breath.

"I've been looking everywhere for you."

Without a glance in her direction, he turned and walked back into the garage. "Ever think maybe I was avoiding you on purpose?" The barbed reply pricked his conscience, but he continued with his task and picked up another box, carrying it back to his truck.

"I. . .I just wanted to know if we could talk."

"Nothing to talk about."

"Well, I've got a few things on my mind. Would you hear me out?"

Alec threw the box into his truck with more force than necessary, startling Lydia. So she'd been right. Gerald had succeeded in tearing them apart. Obviously, Alec had changed his mind about her. . .about them.

"As you can see, I'm kinda busy," he said tersely. "But if it'll make you feel better, then by all means, vent. I'll try to pay attention." He walked back into the garage.

Lydia felt tempted to just walk away and not say another word; however, she somehow sensed that Alec's gruff demeanor was a mask to cover his pain. But could she get through to him—past that steel armor of his?

Lord, I've got one shot here, she quickly prayed. *Please give me wisdom.*

Alec set more items into his truck and then it suddenly occurred to Lydia that he was boxing up the remainder of his belongings.

"Are you going somewhere?"

"Yep." He walked away again.

This time she pursued him into the garage.

He glanced over his shoulder. "I'm leaving Woodruff. In fact, I'm leaving North Carolina."

"I see," Lydia said, fighting the sting of tears. She lifted her chin. "So, you're content with letting Gerald win?"

Alec swung around. "Yeah, he won. Look at me! He's taken everything!"

"You still have the Lord. And you still have me."

He huffed and returned to his sorting and packing.

"As for your job," Lydia continued boldly, "you said it didn't mean more to you than I do. And your house. . . well, the homeowners insurance should cover the loss." She stepped forward and touched his sleeve. "Don't you see, Alec, you lost things. Temporal things. They can be replaced."

"Easy for you to say." He pulled away from her and strode to his truck.

Again, she trailed him. "So this is really it? You're leaving? It doesn't matter to you that we love each other?"

"Lydia," he said, facing her at last, "get real, will you? I love you as much as I could love any human being, but it won't work. I've got nothing to offer you. I can't support myself, let alone a family, and it'll take me years to get back on my feet again. That's too long to wait."

"I'm willing."

"I'm not." He laughed curtly, bitterly. "I dream about you at night, Lydia. Never before has a woman—any woman—affected me the way you do."

"There's a reason," Lydia countered, her face flaming from his candid admission. "We're meant to be together."

"Didn't you hear what I said? No. Now, get out of here!"

"You don't mean that. I know you don't. And we could fight back. . .if you'd only stop feeling sorry for yourself long enough to hear my idea. But if your mind is made up, then there's nothing more I can say."

She wheeled around and walked away, only to pause several strides later. "Alec Corbett, I would have never believed you could be such a. . .*wimp!*"

Spinning on her heel, she continued down his driveway. She heard him slam the door of his truck forcefully, and she couldn't help the satisfied smirk that curled her lips. "Yellow-belly coward!" she called over her shoulder.

That did it. From the corner of her eye, she saw him round his pickup and come after her. She almost laughed out loud. Nothing like insulting a guy's manhood to get his attention! But she nonchalantly kept walking to her car and had almost reached it when Alec grabbed hold of her elbow and whirled her to face him. His hold was surprisingly gentle considering the ferocious expression contorting his handsome features.

"Where's your brain, Lydia?" he asked roughly. "You can't marry a guy like me no matter how much we love each other."

"Are you asking me to marry you?"

"No, because it's out of the question. Can't you see?"

"Well, then, could I ask you? Will you marry me, Alec?"

Beneath the street lamp, she saw a flicker of amusement cross his face. "Sorry, honey, I'm the man and I do the asking."

"In that case, could I interest you in a business proposition?"

Releasing her, Alec folded his arms, looking curious. "What kind of business proposition?"

She set her hands on his thick forearms. "It'll solve everything and we can be together. . .forever." She tipped her head. "Buy me a cup of coffee and let's talk."

❧

"It's a tempting offer," Alec said, sipping his coffee at the Calico Junction restaurant in town. The place had closed at nine, but the owner had been one of Michael's clients and graciously allowed them to sit and talk while he cleaned up the kitchen. Thus, they had the place to themselves. "But I'm not marrying you for your money."

"No, you're marrying me because you love me. And I love you. The money is an added blessing."

He chuckled, the first time all evening.

"Alec, if you don't marry me," she pressed, "just think of the precarious position I'll be in. Word will get out that I've got this trust hanging over my head and awful men like Sim will start crawling out of the woodwork, trying to entice me. Of course, I'll never marry anyone except you, so their efforts will be in vain. . .but what a nuisance. Furthermore, that million dollars will go to waste. I can't touch it unless I remarry."

Alec eyed her speculatively. "You Boswicks sure know how to get to a guy."

"Does that mean yes?" Lydia asked hopefully, drawing

comfort from the lightness of his expression.

"I'll think about it," he said tersely, downing the rest of his coffee.

"Don't think too long. Brian feels my life could be in danger, but I don't really believe it. Nevertheless, the idea upset Mama and Pete enough that they took Tyler and Brooke to the Smiths' in Tennessee. Pete was afraid Gerald might hire someone to kidnap the children and, as a ransom of sorts, I'd have to marry Sim."

Alec paled visibly. "I never thought of that. I guess I've been so focused on myself, I failed to think about you and the kids. I'm so sorry, Lydia."

She set her hand on top of his. "It's understandable."

He looked over at her, his eyes searching her face in uncertainty. "You're too good for me, know that?"

"Oh, don't start. I need you right now." She leaned toward him. "You're my hero, Alec. My knight in shining armor."

"Yeah, and you're my damsel in distress." He grinned, but slowly sobered once again. "I'd like to laugh off the abduction idea, but the fact is, I wouldn't put it past your father-in-law. I mean, if he was desperate enough to firebomb my house, why wouldn't he resort to kidnapping his grandchildren?"

"That's exactly what Pete said."

"And if that's really the case, Tyler and Brooke aren't safe anywhere."

"There's only one solution."

He met her gaze, then took her hand and squeezed it affectionately as they stood. "Come on, let's go talk to Mark Spencer."

While Alec fairly tugged her toward the door of the restaurant, elation filled Lydia's heart. Everything was going to be all right.

epilogue

"Boy, you sure gottalotta junk!"

Standing on the fence beside his best friend, Matt Smith, Tyler nodded as he watched the movers unloading several pieces of furniture. "We filled up the whole truck and my new dad's pickup was bursting with stuff."

"Wow. Good thing you bought the Maxwells' house. It's gottalotta rooms."

"And the best thing is, we get to live next door to each other again!"

"Yeah!"

A few minutes passed and then Tyler looked at his buddy. "What's humble pie?"

Matt shrugged. "I'm not sure, but I think it's got spinach in it and tastes nasty."

"Oh." Tyler mulled over the explanation. "My dad said he had to eat a lot of it before marrying Mama."

"I wonder why."

Tyler shrugged. He'd never understand grown-ups. Except, maybe once he became one, things would make more sense. All he knew was that Mama looked happy all the time, and Mr. Alec was now his dad. In fact, Mr. Alec looked happy all the time, too. And Tyler had been practicing calling him "Daddy," and the name seemed to fit just right. The only bad thing was Daddy's business kept him gone a lot, but Mama promised things would change once they all moved to Tennessee.

After Mama and Mr. Alec got married, he'd gone ahead to Tennessee to "scope things out," only returning home on weekends. Daddy started his own company, building all kinds of furniture and cabinets, and he told Mama, "Business is booming." Daddy said he wanted to start over somewhere new and not long after, he found this house right next to Matt's, bought it, and here they were!

"Hey, Ty," Matt began, "I heard my daddy say your Grampa Boswick is going to jail."

Tyler nodded sadly. "Yep, he did some pretty bad things, but I don't know what exactly."

"Are you gonna visit him ever?"

"Beats me."

"That'd be cool to see the inside of a real jail."

Tyler let the comment go. He wasn't sure if it'd be cool or not. He'd just decided he would rather feel happy that Mama married Mr. Alec—that is, *Daddy*—than feel sad that his grampa messed up. But Daddy said everybody messed up sometimes, and now he and Brooke and Mama all had to forgive and forget.

Suddenly Tyler's parents walked out the back door of their new house with Brooke running after them. Daddy whispered something to Mama and then kissed her long and slow, like he did all the time.

"Yuck," Matt grumbled, his face scrunched up in distaste.

Daddy looked over. "Ty, you want to come to the hardware store with me? Maybe we'll pick up a pizza on the way home."

"Sure!" He never missed a chance to go someplace with his new dad—even if it meant not hanging out with his best friend. "See ya, Matt."

"Yeah, see ya."

Climbing over the fence rail, Tyler jumped down and ran across the lawn. Then he and Daddy made their way to the pickup with Mama and Brooke waving after them. A surge of utter happiness filled Tyler's being. Nothing beat having Matt as his next-door neighbor again, except maybe getting the daddy he'd prayed for. That was awesome!

And just like his best friend, Tyler now had a real family of his own!

A Letter To Our Readers

Dear Reader:

In order that we might better contribute to your reading enjoyment, we would appreciate your taking a few minutes to respond to the following questions. We welcome your comments and read each form and letter we receive. When completed, please return to the following:

Rebecca Germany, Fiction Editor
Heartsong Presents
PO Box 719
Uhrichsville, Ohio 44683

1. Did you enjoy reading *Southern Sympathies?*
   ☐ Very much. I would like to see more books
      by this author!
   ☐ Moderately
      I would have enjoyed it more if _____
      _____
      _____

2. Are you a member of **Heartsong Presents**? Yes ☐ No ☐
   If no, where did you purchase this book?_____
   _____

3. How would you rate, on a scale from 1 (poor) to 5 (superior), the cover design?_____

4. On a scale from 1 (poor) to 10 (superior), please rate the following elements.

   _____ Heroine   _____ Plot

   _____ Hero   _____ Inspirational theme

   _____ Setting   _____ Secondary characters

5. These characters were special because_____

_____

_____

6. How has this book inspired your life?_____

_____

_____

7. What settings would you like to see covered in future **Heartsong Presents** books?_____

_____

_____

8. What are some inspirational themes you would like to see treated in future books?_____

_____

_____

9. Would you be interested in reading other **Heartsong Presents** titles?   Yes ☐   No ☐

10. Please check your age range:
    ☐ Under 18   ☐ 18-24   ☐ 25-34
    ☐ 35-45   ☐ 46-55   ☐ Over 55

11. How many hours per week do you read?_____

Name _____

Occupation _____

Address _____

City _____ State _____ Zip _____

Hearts♥ng Presents
Love Stories Are Rated G!

That's for godly, gratifying, and of course, great! If you love a thrilling love story, but don't appreciate the sordidness of some popular paperback romances, **Heartsong Presents** is for you. In fact, **Heartsong Presents** is the *only inspirational romance book club* featuring love stories where Christian faith is the primary ingredient in a marriage relationship.

Sign up today to receive your first set of four, never before published Christian romances. Send no money now; you will receive a bill with the first shipment. You may cancel at any time without obligation, and if you aren't completely satisfied with any selection, you may return the books for an immediate refund!

Imagine. . .four new romances every four weeks—two historical, two contemporary—with men and women like you who long to meet the one God has chosen as the love of their lives. . . all for the low price of $9.97 postpaid.

To join, simply complete the coupon below and mail to the address provided. **Heartsong Presents** romances are rated G for another reason: They'll arrive *Godspeed!*